For Daniel, my husband, my best friend,
and the reason I believe in happy endings

MOONLIGHT MIST

MIST RIDERS
BOOK FIVE

Stella Fitzsimons

BUTTERFLY ELECTRIC PRESS

MOONLIGHT MIST

The Chronicles of Luna Mae

Whoever fights monsters should see to it that in the process he does not become a monster...

FRIEDRICH NIETZSCHE

Chapter 1

I STARED AT THE announcement pinned on the wall. Apparently, Cyrus had scheduled our wedding for September 5th, just two weeks from now, without bothering to tell me. Classic toxic alpha-male power move. I'd been waiting for something like this since our colossal fight last week when he ordered his goons to move my things to his room—a posh and pompous suite fit for a royal couple. After I put a quick end to that battle, I knew Cyrus would go about finding some feeble method of exacting his revenge.

To be fair, his haste to tie the knot was probably part of a bigger effort to have me stay put in his tacky shifter compound instead of roaming off every chance I got. He must have thought that being my husband would give him some additional leverage to... I don't know, have me redecorate the entire Keep, or participate in the endless uber boring pack council meetings, or maybe take up origami or some other docile bullshit.

I'd grown bolder as the weeks went by. I left the compound almost daily to meet up with Kirsi or Lily or Faion—sometimes all three of them. It drove Cyrus crazy. It drove Darius crazy, too, when Cyrus informed him during one of his weekly reports. At least twice, the Persian King of Kings had chewed me out for taking unnecessary risks.

I shrugged it all off. I knew what they didn't. Horror wasn't going to pop up out of nowhere to wipe me out. He needed me very much alive. He had beheaded Cerber just for trying to hurt me and had eagerly offered to kill Darius as well, and making me his captive would ruin his grand design. Horror intended to lure me to him, so I would willingly become his right hand and openly offer up my mist rider powers to aid in his absolute dominion over all realms.

My gut told me as long as I let Horror believe there was a chance I'd join forces with him, he'd let me be, at least for a while. And for someone as old as Horror, a while could very well mean decades.

I turned around, sensing someone watching. Cyrus stood right behind me, staring intensely. His skin glistened with a post-workout sheen.

"Dude," I said, "why you got to be a creeper? And what's the meaning of this?" I pointed at the bulletin board. "I told you, I need at least one year of..." I searched for a word for this charade. "*Betrothal*."

He grunted. "You need a *whole* year to wiggle out of our agreement?"

I waved him off and stepped away.

I could smell what he ate. *Something raw.*

He liked to shift into a huge black panther at dawn and hunt in the pack's private woods.

"Your non-response concedes the point," he said, licking his lips.

"Men and their imaginary scores," I said, losing interest.

"It's that very agreement that allows your mentor's recuperation to proceed unhindered."

I bit my tongue. I had improved at holding back, never letting anyone know what fevered thoughts raced through my head. The truth was I would do anything to keep Winter safe, even getting hitched to a megalomaniac.

"The pride of a blackmailer," I said.

Cyrus gritted his teeth. "Let's not argue in front of pack members."

"Why? Wouldn't arguing be the best way to pose as a real couple?"

A storm brewed behind his eyes. He motioned me to follow him up three flights of stairs. That wasn't a good sign. His business office was up there, and he hated being in that office. There was something he had to tell me and whenever he had to tell me something, it usually sucked.

His receptionist, a slightly built man for a wolf shifter, stood at attention as we approached. "My alpha, the Chicago pack's been calling all morning—"

Cyrus cut him off with a dry, "Not now."

We entered his large, open office. It was all mahogany and velvet with arched windows overlooking a duck pond. A case of expensive Cuban cigars sat on the heavy desk. Cyrus kicked the door shut.

I jumped straight to offense. "It's fucking bullshit, Cyrus. It's not enough that you took me from my life and forced me to stay in your putrid velvet Xanadu, you also want to monitor my every move and keep me on property all time? Is this some sick form of revenge?"

He glared at me. "Revenge is the wet dream of weaklings. Nothing will change between us after the wedding. Our communication will remain limited to this occasional trading of barbs if that's what you wish. My focus is on the meeting of the five biggest packs in the country at the end of September. There's pressure to realign the territories. I want to negotiate from a position of maximum strength."

"So what? You're going to aim your Lunar witch wife at them like a loaded gun and make them give you what you want, or we'll blow their castles down? That sounds lovely until they enlist their top assassins to take me out."

His voice was dry, emotionless. "Let them try."

"What? *Let them try?* Really? You're not even going to try to lie? Huh," I said. "Maybe I should be grateful you're not hiding the fact that of course, they're going to try to kill me! They're fucking shifter alphas, Cyrus."

"You're a Lunar witch. You're going to be hunted regardless of your circumstances. We might as well offset that risk with a reward."

"Offset this," I said while showing him a middle finger.

Not my best moment. Maturity is not a fixed state.

"You need to grow up," he said. "Life's not an Instagram page. It's not all moral certainties and scented candles. In the real world, shit gets messy."

"You're telling *me* that shit gets messy?" I was stunned. "The same girl who, literally, you and Darius... you know what? Fuck you!"

We had become more than accustomed to these fights. We simmered quietly for a while to let the rage level off.

"Your safety is a priority," he said as some sort of olive branch.

"Right," I said. "I guess that means your security team has been shadowing my every move in and out of the compound. If only you had respected me enough to tell me that."

"I respected you enough that I believed I didn't have to, Sophie. And if you somehow didn't realize you were being followed, that would mean you are clueless enough to need protection."

"Gee, that didn't sound like respect," I said, stating the obvious.

He sighed. "You make me crazy. I actually have a plan and this whole scenario is a pain in my ass as well. I don't have bedside manners, but I'm doing right by you. Trust that."

"Trust is the favorite word of the duplicitous."

He held his eyes closed a long time, biting his lip. "Horror is on the loose and keen on eliminating all competition," he finally said. "Which, I'm not sure why, but Darius thinks you're potentially Horror's nemesis. I promised Darius that you would remain in one piece. I plan on being true to my word."

The bastard sounded sincere. My mind started churning to come up with more stalling tactics to delay the wedding.

"The wedding's happening, Sophie. I suggest you let your people know and be convincing while you're doing it."

Someone, please, kill me now.

My phone buzzed. *Thank God!*

It was a text from Kirsi. She never texted. Her brief *need to talk* message convinced me it was urgent.

I flashed my eyes at Cyrus. "I need to take this. We should both try to be a little more civil to each other."

He shrugged. "Fine."

I hurried up the stairs and texted Kirsi back from my room.

> *Me too. Need yr stealth skills. Meet outside the gate in 1 hr.*

Chapter 2

Kirsi handed me the spare helmet. I held it in my hands, fidgeting with the chin strap.

"That's for your head," she said, arching an eyebrow. "It's human law when riding on two wheels."

I locked my eyes onto hers. "Full disclosure. I have stalkers. The shifting kind. They might be hard to shake."

She batted her impossibly long eyelashes and smiled. "We don't have to shake them. Not yet."

I knew better than to question her assertion and fifteen minutes later, when her Harley-Davidson pulled up to the three-story coffeehouse slash bookstore that belonged to the Society of Immortal Sisterhood, it all became clear. Besides being next to the beauty of Breakwater Way Beach, the shop also allowed us to enter through the front door and exit without being noticed via an elaborate underground network of tunnels.

We sat with a ceramic pot of freshly brewed coffee between us on the second-floor balcony where we could be easily seen from below.

"This is nice," I said.

She took in a deep breath and then slowly let it go. "Agreed. It's good to just sit with a friend."

"That's lovely, though a bit ominous."

"Every bit lovely. Not one bit ominous," she said.

"Happy to hear that," I said. "I'm down with chilling until you're ready to talk about whatever it was you wanted to talk about."

"Really, Luna, it's not a matter of life and death or we'd be having this conversation underground. I'm far more interested in why you find yourself in need of my stealth skills."

"Everyone must ask you for help. You're an Immortal Valkyrie and Guard of the Seventh Council Seal. You make difficult things so much easier. You're like the guy who owns a truck. Every time a friend moves, they'll be calling."

"I also own a truck, so I get that."

Alright then.

"It's about that blackmailing, two-faced dickweed."

"Darius?"

"Nope, the other dickweed, the one who gets in my face every day, making my life a fucking mockery."

"Cyrus? What's he done now on top of everything else?"

"He decided we're getting married in two weeks and announced it to the whole goddamn pack before letting me know," I said.

Kirsi pursed her lips, trying to suppress a laugh.

"Is my tortured existence amusing you?"

"No, it's not that… it's just… that poor bastard really thinks he can command you like some wide-eyed, first-time shifter. I mean, he really doesn't know you And I don't mean Luna the mist rider, I'm talking about Sophie from Astoria, Oregon. Please let me be there when you mount his ass on a wall."

I totally want to mount him on a wall.

I sipped my coffee, saying nothing.

"Luna? End this charade already. I can't let you marry that cretin."

I shrugged. "Unless I find another way to ensure Winter's recovery, what choice do I have?"

Kirsi banged her fist on the table. "For centuries I've seen women forced into unwanted, degrading marriages. Enough."

"It's not real, it's a means to an end. And maybe there won't be a marriage at all if you and I…"

Kirsi raised her hand. "Say no more. I'm all in."

I exhaled and smiled. "Oh, Kirsi… that's music to my ears. I need to find Winter and I can't do that with a bunch of furballs on my trail."

I waved to Marlon in sunglasses down on the beach. His tattoos and muscles were as recognizable as his face. He was the head of Cyrus's security team as well as a frightening wolf, but now he was relegated to trailing me, a job he no doubt hated. He waved back at me as he knocked back cans of Heineken beer along with two of the pack's younger hyenas.

Kirsi rolled her eyes. "That's just sad. Could they be less discreet?"

"I think they give zero fucks at this point. It's a shit assignment. Trailing their boss's fiancée. I almost feel for them."

"Bullshit. Let them bake in the sun. They're unprofessional. This is going to be too easy… where's the fun in that?"

We laughed.

I furrowed my brow at Kirsi. "Your turn. What about that text you sent?"

She sipped her coffee. "It's a touch weird."

"Really? I can do weird. It's kind of my brand. Go ahead, try me."

"I received a message."

"A message? Like a text? Voicemail?"

"A whiteboard message," she said. "On my fridge."

"Your fridge?"

"Yeah, I had a casserole in the oven and went up to take a shower," Kirsi said. "When I came back, I took the casserole out and then I noticed the message written in green erasable marker on my whiteboard. And they erased my little grocery reminders."

"That *is* weird," I said. "I'm stunned actually. I can't believe Valkyries bake casseroles."

"Since long before they were called casseroles."

"Okay, yeah, but breaking into your place and writing on your fridge board," I said. "*You have a fridge board?* Okay. What did it say?"

"Well," she said, "I presume you're aware of Helen and Christian?"

A sudden chill crept up my spine. Why would Kirsi speak the name of Winter's ex-girlfriend and their baby? I was afraid to ask.

I nodded. "Yes, I'm aware."

A shadow crossed Kirsi's face. "According to the note, their death was not an accident. A detail had been over-looked because no one suspected murder."

I stared through her, a heat rising in my chest. "You're saying they were murdered... Helen and little baby Christian?" I said, the words sticky in my mouth as if coated with glue.

Kirsi placed her hand on mine. "We can't know for sure. According to the note, the cab driver who picked up Helen and the baby was female, which was uncommon in San Diego in the fifties."

"Sure, Winter mentioned that. He even remembered her name."

"Poor man," Kirsi said, taking a moment. "The thing is, this woman, *Susan*, replaced the original cab driver at the last moment. She paid the cabbie to let her drive."

I chewed on that. "All this was on your whiteboard? How do we know it's true and *what...* she drove into the lake on purpose, killing herself, not to mention an infant and a nursing mother? Winter would have sensed all this. It's too nefarious. There's no way he'd miss that."

"I'm just relaying the message. It implied if we follow the Susan clue, we'll find out what really happened."

I pressed the back of my head with both hands. "It's a setup, Kirsi. That's all this is, right?"

Kirsi put her hand on mine. "Most probably, but when people try to set me up, I like to play along a little until I can make them pay. And, if there's a single chance there's any truth to this, I want to know that, too."

I pulled my hand back and steeled myself. "Let's fucking do it."

"Shouldn't you be preparing for a wedding, bridezilla?"

"Don't remind me," I said. "If nothing else, this will be a diversion from all that gross nonsense."

Kirsi grinned. "Promise me that if this leads us to Winter somehow, I get to be the one who chops off Darius's head."

"As long as I get to feed it to the demon hounds."

She stood up. "I won't stand between you and your dreams. Now let's go dig into a seventy-year-old cold case and Susan, our *person of interest*."

Did we just become a dynamic detective duo?

We trotted downstairs to the coffee shop. On the patio outside, Eir, the Valkyrie who fought by our side against the necromancers in Nightwood, lay on a lounge chair in a tiny bikini. *Yikes.* Next to her sat none other than Chazona, the ice queen herself: tall, curvy, blonde and pretty in a fucked up, *freeze you to the bone* sort of way. Her eyes flashed a ruthless glee.

"What's that bitch doing here?" I said.

"She's friends with Eir. Don't make a scene, Luna."

I laughed. "As if I would give her the satisfaction."

Kirsi grabbed my hand. "Cellar, now."

She dragged me away. I took one last look at the chilliest and most complete bi—*uh-uh, forget it. I'm above that.*

Chazona's lips curved into a small laugh as she waved to me.

"No! No," Kirsi said. "That's exactly the kind of thing we need to avoid."

I resisted all my instincts to scream obscenities when Chazona waltzed through the door after us. The joy on her arrogant lips was gone, her stare dripping with disdain.

She walked right up to me and bitch-slapped me so hard I fell into Kirsi. And a good thing she was there, or I would have suffered the indignity of falling onto my ass.

"Do you want to die right now?" I said, rubbing my cheek. "What the hell was that for?"

Chazona exhaled. Her eyes glared. "Don't play innocent, you hussy twat. You know that was for Winter. And there's infinite more of *that* coming your way, so put up one of your hocus-pocus defenses for all the good it will do you, little whining witch."

Eir walked next to Chazona. "Ladies," she said. "I've seen

both of you fight. And it's not going to be good for the bookstore."

I'll melt Chazona's brains all over the Feng Shui books.

I glanced at Kirsi. She shook her head, barely.

"What are you talking about?" I said. "Has something happened besides you being a psycho? Is there news of Winter?"

"You're intolerable," she said. "I'm clueless what anyone sees in you. Winter would be fine right now if you weren't slinking around him every waking moment batting your pathetic eyelashes, and you know it."

What's wrong with my eyelashes?

"So, you're blaming me for what happened to Winter?"

"Is there anyone who doesn't? Of course, I hold you responsible for a good man almost getting torn apart *and* for him being gone. It's all on little miss, *oh, I'm just a baby witchling who can't possibly be blamed for anything.*"

"I don't know what you want me to say. You're obviously seeing everything in jealous vision."

Eir grabbed Chazona's hand before she could slap me again.

"Why do I even bother?" she said. "Winter was never the same after he crossed paths with you, he became reckless, unfocused, he put a distance between himself and his kind, betrayed his own council, and for *what?* For a coquettish college girl who can't get her tiny head out of her own skinny ass. Now Horror has him—because you had to go and provoke Horror!"

You need to check your sources!

"And who told you all that? Düsternis?"

"You're not exactly denying it."

Of course, it was Düsternis.

"The Grand Magistrate lied to you," I said. "I expect it wasn't the first time he has, because you're all icy bitch and no sense. I had nothing to do with it, Chazona. You get a pass for whatever the fuck this was, but if you lay a finger on me again, it'll be the last thing you ever do."

Chazona laughed. "I can't be killed, you dope."

Kirsi stepped in front of me, sword drawn to face Chazona. "There are things worse than death, Immortal."

I placed my palm on Kirsi's shoulder. "Let's just go, Kirsi."

Chazona and I exchanged a final glance Her nostrils flared. She had really bought Düsternis's deceit, *hook, line and sinker*, and she wasn't the only one. The entire Seventh Council must have been of one mind, blaming me for Winter's current state, but my hands were tied, I could not tell them the truth, because Darius the Undestroyable was blackmailing me.

We ran downstairs to the cellar. Kirsi slid the wooden table out of the way and rolled up the carpet. She unlocked the trapdoor and we descended into the ancient tunnel.

Chapter 3

WE STOOD IN FRONT of the small, shabby corner office that housed the San Diego branch of the Seventh Council digitized media archives. I'd lived in San Diego for almost five years—hell, I'd even walked into the infamous Seventh Council Magistrate Courts more than once—and I had no idea that place existed.

The council effectively hid the office's true nature from the basic world. The beige walls were stained with soot, the glass in a front window was cracked and sealed with green duct tape. The sign on the metal door was a faded orange, and several letters had worn away, making the sign read like gibberish: *NO ARY'S O FICE CLOS D UNTI FU T ER NOTI E.*

This whole cover was *a lot.* Immortal councils never went to all that trouble. They kept their business hidden in Arctic vaults or subterraneous catacombs, away from prying eyes.

It would have been less surprising if Kirsi had taken me to archives on the moon than right here, in the heart of San Diego.

"Hard to believe we can just walk in here and find a clue," I said.

Kirsi shrugged. "The seventh has scanned and catalogued a ton of past newspaper clippings in which a council member's name appeared. And Winter isn't just any old council member. He's been Chief Magistrate for centuries. I'm sure they'll have more than a few on record."

My hand buzzed as I reached for the door.

"Don't," Kirsi commanded.

I stopped my hand six inches from the handle. Invisible Immortal wards. I felt them sense my etheric essence and activate. Their vibrations penetrated my skin, pinching into muscle and tendon.

A pale gold sparked, making me jump back with a shudder. This derelict building would have fried me on the spot had I moved one inch closer.

Kirsi chanted a few incomprehensible sounds. The tickling vanished as the wards hummed harmlessly. Kirsi opened the metal door.

We walked into a small lobby with stone walls. A narrow corridor stretched ahead. We followed it to an unexpected large hall. Bright lights came on one after the other with each step we took. The building seemed to expand out into adjacent constructions.

The walls were lined with shelves crowded with manuals and folded maps, two large wall-to-ceiling windows were boarded up with metal planks, and the row of desks across the hall sported state-of-the-art computers.

Unlike the grungy exterior of the building, the interior was pristine and housed an impressive network of database servers.

Kirsi walked to a computer and quickly scrolled through the archives until she landed on past issues of San Diego newspapers from July of 1956.

She tapped her fingernail on the screen when she came upon July 17. "Luna, before we do this and open Pandora's box, are you completely sure?"

I'm rarely sure about anything.

I began to read the headline on the screen out loud.

CAB STRUCK IN HIT AND RUN SINKS INTO LAKE MURRAY, 3 KILLED

There were only a few small items after that. A dry, trite piece about the tragedy that shook the local community and how there should be better guard rails in place to prevent future accidents. But in that last piece there was a full name of the cab driver included. *Susan Rigby.*

Kirsi gave me a sideways glance. "It mentions her family. A husband and two young sons."

It had been 65 years. They could be anywhere by now. Her husband likely passed long ago. Her sons, if we could find them, were too young in 1956 to have any useful information.

Kirsi's fingers danced on the keyboard. The screen went completely dark. When it sprang back to life, a sequence of blue code spilled down.

"You did something," I said.

"Uh huh," Kirsi said with a chuckle. "I find that *something* is much better to do than *nothing*."

I realized we were going down this rabbit hole for more reasons than to distract me and meet my curiosity about what happened to Helen and the son she had with Winter. Kirsi loved playing detective. Solving mysteries was her true element. Going after bad guys was how she got her kicks.

A list of names flickered on the screen. Kirsi worked fast, eliminating names until there were only two left: Thomas and Franklin Rigby.

"Susan's children," Kirsi said. "Look, Franklin still lives in San Diego."

Whatever network she had plugged into had access to a fully detailed account of Franklin Rigby's life. I skimmed through the basics: 71 years old, a retired Professor of English who had published two books, one about Bach and the other about French impressionists. He had fathered three children. Two daughters and a son.

I reached for my phone.

Kirsi reached out to take my hand. "You don't call. That gives them too easy of an out. He'll refuse to see us. In person, people are more polite, more accommodating."

She had me wait inside while she scanned the area outside to make sure we weren't followed.

"We're good. The coast is clear," she said.

The motorcycle tilted and swerved through light San Diego traffic until slowing to a stop outside a welcoming, Mediterranean style house with a red-tiled roof, arched windows and ocean blue shutters.

Susan's son lived only four blocks from the coffee shop where I had worked for two years. The possible answer to the mysterious deaths of Winter's family hung in the very air I breathed all that time.

We walked up to the double door and rang the bell. A woman in her thirties dressed in pink sweats came to the door. Her brown hair was pulled back into a ponytail, not a single hair astray, a few beads of sweat lingering on her forehead.

"May I help you?" she said.

"We want to speak to Professor Rigby," Kirsi said. "Is he home?"

The woman blinked as she furrowed her brow.

I elbowed Kirsi's ribs to let me do the talking. The Valkyrie lacked a certain tact at times.

"Hi, I'm Sophie Collinsworth," I cut in, "and this is my colleague, Kirsi. We're doing exit research for San Diego

State. Our job is to interview tenured faculty who chose early retirement. Professor Rigby hasn't responded to our emails which leads us to believe we have an old address."

The woman nodded. "I'm Lorraine, the professor's daughter. Mom's been under the weather, so I popped over to lend a hand."

"I'm sorry, if this is the wrong time we can come back."

Lorraine pushed the door wide open. "Not at all. Come on in, dad could use the distraction."

We followed Lorraine into a bright, spacious living room. French doors opened to a long breezeway outside.

"A moment," Lorraine said softly, then vanished out the French doors. She returned accompanied by a distinguished older man.

Franklin Rigby tread cautiously, like he was at risk of stumbling at any moment, yet his large dark eyes flashed self-assurance, even superiority.

He skipped introductions. "When Lorraine informed me that functionaries were here from the college, I did not expect to find two enchanting young beauties in my sitting room. Exactly why are you ladies wasting the very peak of your vibrance on such tedium?"

Kirsi lit up. His chauvinistic charm was something she must still enjoy from all the cringy centuries gone by.

The professor went on. "I shall not waste any more of your time. I retired because I'd grown sick of my own self-absorbed pursuit of academia and my ever-more-rigid intellectualism. So much life drained away in pursuit of the dead husks of past knowledge. I'd had my fill. I could no longer stifle burgeoning minds with musty old ideas."

Ah, that's all bluster and little sense, but okay.

I sighed. "Cards on the table. We are not from the university. We have a much more personal reason to speak with you."

A wide grin formed on his lips. "A spot of intrigue. Now we're getting somewhere."

Lorraine flashed him a look of concern. "Dad, I don't think—"

The professor dismissed her with a wave of his hand. "Don't mind my well-meaning daughter. She adheres to a strictly rational universe. Reason and logic are the twin pillars of her days. Please, my dears, make yourselves comfortable and dazzle me with your unexpected purpose."

"It's about your mother's death," Kirsi said.

He frowned. "My mother? How peculiar." He turned to Lorraine. His frown disappeared. "Now there. You didn't see that coming, did you, my practical daughter?"

Lorraine rolled her eyes. "What possible interest is my grandmother's accident in the 1950s to you?"

"We have reason to believe that was no accident," I said.

The professor furrowed his brow. "Two cars colliding is the very definition of an accident."

Kirsi graced him with a hint of menace. "Exactly, it was the very definition of an accident. Not to be questioned by anyone. What better result could there be for one attempting to stage an accident?"

The playfulness drained from his face. "Staged? What fiend would go to such heinous lengths to murder two innocent women and a small child? You have both wasted your time and for what? Injecting evil intent into decades old tragedies?"

I shook my head. "You misunderstand, the last thing we're suggesting is that your mother played any intentional part in this. There was more likely a setup of some sort. The other woman and the baby, you might have guessed, were part of our family."

Kind of, sort of... okay, not really.

Kirsi leaned forward. "We just want to know if your late mother was a cab driver by profession."

"No, no, she wasn't."

"Then why was she behind the wheel of that cab?" I said.

The professor shut his eyes. "You understand, I was six at the time," he said, becoming fragile. "How I wish they had never let me see her body. She was picture-perfect, unblemished, like a sleeping angel." He hung his head as if feeling it all again. "Years later, I asked my father this very question."

We waited for him to collect himself. Even after all these years, the memories were still raw.

His daughter put her hand on his shoulder.

"He said she was doing a favor for a friend."

"Is there anything else you can tell us?" I said. "Anything

that wasn't in the newspapers?"

He looked at me but was really looking back through the veil of time.

Lorraine's cheeks flushed. "Dad, don't."

Kirsi scoffed. "Clearly, you're hiding something."

"It's not like that, it's not even about the accident," Lorraine said. "It's a private family matter."

The professor put his hand on his daughter's hand. "There's no shame in it, Lorraine." He turned back to us. "Our money. It comes from my mother."

"How is that significant?" I said.

"At the time of her death my mother was terminally ill," he said. "She only had months to live, maybe a year."

"I'm very sorry," I said.

"And the money," Kirsi said, "how does that play in?"

The professor inhaled, his nostrils flaring. "Days later, perhaps it was a week, my father informed us that weeks before her death, my mother had inherited money from the rich English uncle who had raised her. Some three-hundred thousand dollars. My father put much of it into the Mission Bay development project, buying up land. Imagine, my dear girls, what owning prime California real estate has done over 65 years."

"I can't even imagine," I said.

He nodded. "My parents meant to tell my brother and me together, they had been planning a family trip to Paris, maybe the last with my mother... a trip we never took. My father mourned her death the rest of his days."

An obvious cover story, even the old man felt it.

"The problematic timing," Kirsi said. "Is that why it's a secret?"

"A man living in such pain could not stomach all the intrigue that would have undoubtedly arisen in whispers about the ill-timed fortune arriving amidst tragedy. We left. He took us to England for a time, then Chicago before returning to San Diego six years later."

I resisted the urge to speak freely. "We appreciate your candor. It seems as if everything checks out, it was a tragic accident. Thank you for understanding our creative approach to meeting with you."

"I have another word for that," Lorraine said, quite through with us.

The professor stood, his face pale and his lips pursed. There were no goodbyes. We made our way to the door with Lorraine at our heels. She shut the door behind us just as quick as she could.

Kirsi's eyebrows lifted. "Tell me you didn't buy an ounce of that drivel?"

"No," I said. "And neither do they, although they pretend for each other, just as the others in the family have pretended since 1956."

"So *sick Susan* allowed herself to be offed for money," Kirsi said. "And became a double murderer in the process. I'd like to go back in time and suffocate her with her own delusional sense of nobility."

"Kirsi, come on, that's not helping."

"It would help me," she said, completely serious.

"Well, that ship has sailed," I said. "I want to catch whoever it was that put her up to it. Someone who had that kind of money shouldn't be too hard to trace."

"If they were an adult then," Kirsi said, "what makes you sure they are still alive now?"

"Don't play games, Kirsi. We both know the person behind this was not of mortal birth. And don't give me shit about profiling."

"Fine, but I'm not sure we're going to like what we find out."

"We're not going to live with our heads in the sand," I said. "Stop playing these word games, you're a Valkyrie, grow a pair."

Not anatomically correct, but she got it.

"Okay, *sis*, then we have to follow the money."

"Obviously, we follow the money," I said. "I've watched TV dramas before."

"Fine," Kirsi said. "Well, I know it from the real world. So, I'll just go back to the Seventh's archives to do that now. Are we mad at each other?"

I closed my eyes and exhaled all my frustrations. "No, *Kirs*, it's not you. I love you. I'm just mad at the world right now. I feel sick. Hey, I'm only a few blocks from my apartment. I'm going to walk there."

"I get it," she said, grabbing my shoulders and peering into my eyes. "Chin up, moon child."

She jumped on her bike and took off like a rocket.

Chapter 4

Nothing had changed in my studio apartment. Same pistachio walls, same Persian rug, same velvety chocolate couch, same clothes splayed where they didn't belong. The only thing that had changed since the last time I was here was me and that made everything feel off.

I hadn't been back to my place in over two months. It would be easy to say it was because Cyrus had demanded I stayed at the shifter compound, but that would not be entirely true. The truth is I never wanted to return to the place where Winter had laid next to me in bed, skin on skin, his heart pounding against mine as we fell asleep on the eve of setting out for Nightwood and the battle against Horror's army—a battle that nearly claimed Winter's life.

Standing in my own home brought a physical anguish. With every breath my chest hurt. I missed him. And I knew it would get worse when the adrenaline from my revenge dreams died out and I was left alone and unsure if Winter would ever recover.

And if he did, would he ever be the same?

The only bright spot was that Cyrus should be seething by now. No matter what, that made all of this worth it, to make the bastard stew in his own arrogance for a while.

When the phone rang later, I was standing at the window, peeking outside through the blinds.

"Hey, Kirsi," I said, "any news?"

"*It's not good, I'm afraid. All information pertaining to Susan's finances has been wiped clean. All gone, poof, vanished.*"

"Of course," I said pensively. "Whoever hired her made sure of erasing anything that could connect them to the murder."

"*We had to try. And we'll keep trying.*"

"Why?" I said. "We're at a dead end. We only had one clue."

"*You are a terrible detective. It's a dead end, it's not THE end. There are other ways to get that information. It takes time.*"

Time was exactly what I didn't have.

I tried not to sound deflated. "I'll just follow your lead."

"*Still at your apartment?*"

"Uh huh."

"*See you shortly.*"

My life was nothing but a series of setbacks. Going

through proper channels would take ages and I didn't have ages. I had two weeks. Barely. We could go back and ask the professor, but it'd be hard to do that without raising his suspicions.

I heard a knock on the door. It was too soon to be Kirsi. Most probably it was Marlon or another member of his security team. *Shit.* As long as it wasn't Cyrus himself, because that would blow.

I pulled the door open to find a tall man I'd never seen before holding a black leather briefcase. I figured him to be in his early forties. He wore an elegant navy-blue suit and a white collared shirt unbuttoned at the top. His broad shoulders and perfect posture emanated self-assurance. His close-cropped hair appeared strawberry blond as did his tightly trimmed beard. He had a sophisticated appeal. His handsome linear face and dark green eyes held a sharp but pleasant gaze.

Definitely not a shifter.

I stared at him. "Hi."

He unleashed a preloaded charming smile, never a good sign. "Good afternoon, Miss Collinsworth."

He's too dressed up to be a cable guy. This has to be life insurance.

"I'm not a salesperson," he assured me. I detected a slight Northern European accent. Not Scandinavian, but something thereabouts. "I'm the legal counsel for Professor Franklin Rigby."

Hold the phone.

"The professor? How did you even find me?"

"He gave me your name and mentioned the university."

"Right," I said. "What's this about?"

The man offered me his business card. *Milan Visser... Dutch maybe?*

"Might I step inside? It's a private matter."

I opened the door and stepped aside. He lingered outside, scanning my apartment with an unnerving intensity.

"Have a seat," I said, prodding him to enter and sit on the couch.

He elegantly unbuttoned his blazer, popped open his briefcase and pulled out a simple manila folder. I remained on my feet.

"My client wishes to aid you in your search, pursuant an agreement that any assistance he might offer shall remain confidential. No persons, not even his children, can know of his participation."

"Agreed."

"Noted. So, we shall proceed. My client has secured his mother's journal in a safety deposit box at the location of the California Bank & Trust at 525 B Street, right here in San Diego."

He handed me a small key. The whole thing felt like a movie.

"My client believes the journal will be of some use to you. He specifically suggests you pay close attention to page 36.

Professor Rigby is at the bank now authorizing you to have access to the deposit box. Your signature and a photo ID are all you need at the counter to unlock the box."

He pulled a tablet from his briefcase and instructed me to sign a bank form on the screen.

"Good. I have just transferred this to the bank. Task complete."

I noticed his signet ring engraved with odd, overlapping red letters or symbols. It was calligraphy and indecipherable to my eyes.

He returned the tablet to the briefcase and handed me a piece of paper. "That's a note from Professor Rigby. He wishes to have no further contact with you in any form. You are not to visit him, call him or email him. Any questions you might have should be addressed to me directly."

I unfolded the piece of paper. There were only two unsteadily written words in green ink. *Good luck.*

"I guess that's that."

"Indeed," Milan Visser said. He rose to pat down his pants and extend a hand.

We shook. He held onto my hand longer than good manners would dictate.

"A true pleasure doing business with you, Miss Collinsworth. I'm sure our paths will cross again. Wishing you all good fortune."

Okay, that was a little cringe.

The ten minutes I waited for Kirsi lasted forever.

"Dude," I told her. "Where've you been? I got a lead."

WE SAT WITH OUR lattes between us at the Starbucks across from the bank. Kirsi was completely transfixed by Susan's journal. When we first took the journal from the deposit box, I sensed a foul presence scraping against my etheric essence. Magic gathered into my hands ready to strike, but the sensation subsided.

The entry on page 36 of the journal was unsettling.

> *It will happen anyway. I determine nothing. I just drive. I do nothing. I drive. Someone has to drive. The darkness is preset. My life will be pain and purgatory. My family broken. That seals my fate. Their fate is already sealed, poor souls. I author no ill will. Let it be me. Let another driver live. Let me be released... from my hell... from my bitter end. My family will yet flourish. They will call this the hand of God and so it will be... for I determine nothing.*

Susan Rigby was tortured by an unthinkable choice. She was already dying. She was worried about her family's future. She was possibly coerced. That bought no sympathy from me. She was clearly not capable of preventing anything, sure, but that did not excuse her actions. She was a villain. Plain and simple. The money she earned for her family had been a curse and a burden through all these years.

She willingly played a role in the death of a young woman and her baby. Any way you unpacked that, she would always be a fiend.

Had the professor been given the journal on his father's deathbed, or had it been found among his possessions during the settling of his estate? No matter how or when it came into the professor's hands, it must have been a most appalling discovery.

In his shoes, I'd have immediately given all that blood money to charity, but people deal with things in different ways. I was in no position to judge.

"Anything specific we can use?" I said, reminding Kirsi I was there.

Kirsi started to speak before being interrupted by a chilling shriek. Cars skidded to a halt, panicked pedestrians collided and found cover. Others froze in place or started snapping photos of some startling thing I could not see.

Kirsi jumped up and jogged to the street. The driver of a black sedan sprinted away from his car in the opposite direction. I followed Kirsi. My jaw fell to the floor. Down the street, a gigantic ancient Earth troll loomed in front of Symphony Towers. His head reached almost halfway up the huge tower complex. That motherfucker might have been a hundred feet tall. Or more.

"Holy shit," Kirsi said.

Holy shit on steroids! Earth trolls had roamed the magic world tens of thousands of years ago until the Eternals banished them to a special wing of the exile vortex. They were the largest supernatural creatures to have ever roamed the five realms. They could topple fortresses with their stout legs, and they wore gigantic armor plates that could shoot out steel spikes the size of warheads. Earth trolls could not process rational thought, they didn't form bonds of any kind, they knew no mercy, honored no boundaries, and were driven exclusively by instinct, hunger and blood lust.

Their banishment was supposed to be permanent yet here we were, staring one in its ugly mega mug in the heart of San Diego. Smart phones filming away, no doubt a few Facebook live feeds being transmitted to the entire globe.

The Earth troll roared. His dry, warbling voice reverberated off buildings, drowning out all human noises. Then he quietly licked his gross lips.

A young woman shrieked. "Somebody, call the police!"

Kirsi turned to me. "I think it might have just eaten the police."

A lump formed in my throat. "What do we do?"

Kirsi's face went dark. "I don't even have my sword."

An idea erupted into my head. "There's a ley line intersection behind Balboa Stadium. I feel it. If I can somehow draw the ley line energy to me without the troll noticing, I might possibly be able to contain him."

The Earth troll grunted as he pivoted to the right. He seemed unsure what to do, dazed and confused maybe. My gut told me he was dragged or dropped into the basic world and had no idea how he got here.

I had to act before the beast got its bearings. Problem was, if the stories at the Lunar Order school were true, Earth trolls could innately detect even the slightest of energy transfers. Although they couldn't command ley line energy, they sensed when others drew on it to fight them. Calling all that raw power to me was like sending an invitation out to have my head bashed in. There was no way I'd outrun the troll if he sensed my ley line manipulation.

Kirsi read my mind. "Do it," she said. "I'll keep him dancing."

She pulled a dagger from her boot and charged down the street. Valkyries are basically lunatics.

The troll stepped forward. The earth shook. Flames shot from his nostrils.

Good lord.

It took me one breath to locate the ley lines and another to lock onto a multiplicity of energy currents. It felt like climbing onto a tidal wave and losing all control of my own power reserves.

My body strained as I smashed into an invisible barrier that blocked my access to the ley lines. I struggled to get a new hold, every bit of my core aching, when the world slowed down around me. The screams of the basics faded and all that was left was the pounding of my pulse in my ears. My body felt light as if floating. I could hear my eyelids blinking.

Every moving thing, including the troll, froze in place.

The fuck? Has time halted?

Only Chronomasters could pull off this trick and they were banned from the basic world. The impact of halting time here could be devastating.

A shooting pain erupted in my skull and with it a deep, echoing voice born out of my trembling magic core.

"Daughter of mine, do you need protection?"

Fucking hell. How did he penetrate my shields again?

"Did you do this?" I thought through blinding pain. "Did you freeze time?"

"No. Time stopped by the same hand that released the troll."

"Thanks, Dad, now crawl back into whatever dark asshole of the universe you've been hiding."

His raspy voice persisted. "This is no time for angst. What can I do?"

"Hmm," I said, "how about boil your heart and eat it?"

"Don't let the city fall to spite me." His voice sounded almost human now. It infuriated me that he was right. I couldn't reach the ley line energy and I'd never sacrifice the city I loved or any city.

"Fine, you can use your toxic male powers to wipe clean the memories of all basics who saw or even heard of the Earth troll anywhere in the world."

A wave of unbridled energy washed over me, turning my limbs into goo. My head swam in a pool of intoxicating power. My own etheric core buzzed as it bonded with the power of my father.

"Done," the voice said. "The last ten minutes never happened in the minds of any of the billions of measly surface dwellers."

Damn. How infinite was his power?

"Now hurry up, child, we don't know when the hidden puppeteer will unfreeze time."

I looked at the troll. His tongue hung out of his mouth, trapped between rows of sharp, monstrous teeth. His left foot was suspended a few feet above a pizza delivery truck.

"I don't want to kill the troll."

"You are the daughter of time, progeny of the Great Master of Eternal and Perpetual Creatures and Keeper of all living realms. Use the power in your blood, forge your eternal heritage to force the ancient creature back into banishment. You control all time and space portals, my flower."

I do what now? What's he on about?

"How do you think your mongrel brother travels? I handed him the keys to the time portals ages ago."

So, that's how Chaos does it? He's like a magic trust fund baby.

"I am giving you the same power, daughter. Only the Master of Time can gift the vanishing smoke. Consider it a token of my goodwill. Now focus, see what is right in front of you."

I squinted against the harsh sunlight. A rippling curtain of dancing light flickered in the distance behind the massive troll. The curtain contracted and then expanded again with clockwork precision.

The time portal.

It was luminous. It took my breath away. A strange tear watered the corner of my eye. I felt such awe and yet it felt familiar.

I gathered up all my magic and exploded it out through my fingertips toward the time portal. The shimmering lights twirled into a whirlwind and swelled, responding to my call. The portal opened wide and sucked the Earth troll suddenly into its grasp. He disappeared with a loud cracking pop.

The lights vanished, the portal closed.

"All in a day's work," the voice said. "We make a good team."

The pressure in my head abated. Horror left me.

I fell into a dark void. When I came to, the world had returned to normal. Confused people staring at cars abandoned in the street were the last sign that anything had happened.

Kirsi walked back to me, perplexed. "Where'd you bounce that troll to?"

I shrugged. "Not sure, I guess I got lucky."

Shit. Penelope had warned me about this. Horror would

find a way to tempt me, to bond with me, to make me not want to kill him. I had an uneasy feeling that I had been duped, that my estranged and very dangerous father had orchestrated this whole scheme, a stupid con game called *Hide the Troll*.

Chapter 5

THE PERSISTENT BANGING WAS so forceful I thought the door would come off its hinges. I opened one eye to peek at the clock on the nightstand. It was after two in the morning. Who in the hell was trying to wake up half of the Keep?

I slipped on a tank top and sweats and went to the door. Darius, fabled commander of the Ten Thousand Immortals, glared at me before stomping into my room with Cyrus in tow.

"Let me guess," I said. "You want me to paint the turrets before the wedding, right? Or maybe a hot new design for the napkins?"

Darius grabbed me by the shoulders and sat me down. He was cleanly shaven and dressed casual for the first time since I'd met him.

Fury colored his dark eyes. "What dangerous games have you been playing, witch?" he hissed.

I laughed. "I don't know. Plants vs Zombies."

"Everything's a joke to you," he said. "Tell us what you were doing at the intersection of B street and 7th Avenue yesterday afternoon?"

How the hell did he know?

"What intersection? Try asking the Cyrus goon squad. They follow me everywhere 24/7. I'm sure they keep a log. They'll know whether I was getting a coffee or donut or, god forbid, both."

Cyrus impatiently shook his head. "Come off it, Sophie. He's already been briefed you shook my security team earlier in the day."

"We know there was a colossal paranormal phenomenon happening there," Darius said. "And an unprecedented residual magic load was detected moments later by the psychic orbs."

"Wow. I wish I had been there to see all that."

Darius took on a murderous expression. "Once again, you try my patience. Your energy signature was all over that magic. And it all lines up nicely with you losing your security detail. Then promptly a dormant time portal unseals for the first time in ten millennia and spits out something dark and ancient before resealing moments later."

I chuckled. "Because I'm a big opener and closer of dormant time portals. I'm famous for that and my oatmeal cookie recipe."

Darius leaned forward, looked straight into my eyes and

said in a barely audible low tone, "You might fool basics or even shifters with your paltry wit, but your wordplay has no effect on me."

"You're barking up the wrong tree, Darius. No offense, Cyrus," I said. "Maybe you should be more concerned about that portal opening and big ass trolls running loose in San Diego!"

Darius grinned. "That's funny. I never mentioned a troll."

I'm so busted.

"Fine," I said. "I was trying not to show off. Yes, I happened to be in the area, which is one of my normal hangout areas. Did you expect me to sit back and watch the Earth troll crush hundreds of people and cause a worldwide meltdown of the basics' understanding of existence? I tried to contain him, but I failed. Whoever unleashed the troll in San Diego was the one who sucked it back into the portal. I was just a frightened bystander like everyone else."

"That's a rather convenient version of the events," Darius said.

"No, it's not. I failed. Simple as that," I said. "You can't just throw that phrase out when what happened doesn't match the version you literally just made up in your head. Use your little army of fanboys and find out who is actually trying to erase the line that keeps the two worlds separated."

Cyrus arched an eyebrow. "Would that be so terrible?"

"Yeah, Cyrus. This way it would. Perhaps if there was a gradual process agreed upon by all parties, but unleashing an

Earth troll upon basics is definitely not it."

Cyrus nodded. "So, we lose the troll."

"You're not funny," I said.

Okay, maybe a little funny.

Darius looked at Cyrus with disdain, likely concerned his godson had gone soft on me.

Guess what, I don't need to see your alpha male pissing contest.

My phone buzzed. *Thank god!* A text from Faion.

> **Crazy town down in the DD, moon lune. Real fugly monster madness. Fights etc. etc. Dropping by your crib in the a.m. with deets.**

"You look forlorn," Darius said. "Bad news?"

Think quick, girl. Come on.

"Ah, it's my apartment, the building manager," I said. "There was a leak in my unit. I need to check out the damage in the morning."

"Cyrus will put his people on it."

I shook my head. "Like hell. I'm not going to have a bunch of furball stalkers going through my panty drawer. It's my home, I'll handle it."

"*This* is your home now," Darius said.

"Huh," I said. "No matter how many times you say it, it'll never make it true. Listen, the goons can stand outside, but I'm definitely going. Now, please leave my room. Yeesh, dudes are exhausting."

As soon as they left, a new kind of wariness nibbled at me. So, if Horror's memory spell didn't affect a demigod like Darius, what other Immortals and Eternals had sensed my control of the time portal? Had the master orb in the Deep Down registered my etheric essence? I had zero insights into any of it and that left me feeling uneasy.

Marlon parked the car a block away. He led me to the apartment building through a back alley I didn't know existed. I wasn't about to argue with him since he was already beyond pissed. Cyrus must have given him an earful for losing me yesterday.

We took the stairs to the second floor. Marlon halted a few steps away from my apartment door. He brought his index finger to his mouth.

I stopped cold in my tracks, wondering what it was that had given his super-sharpened wolf senses pause. Was it a routine thing, or did he sense something was off?

He sniffed at the air, drawing a gun out.

Oh shit.

I mouthed *what the hell are you doing.* He pointed at the door, pretending to tap on it a few times. He thought someone was inside my apartment.

Before I had a chance to tell him it was probably a friend,

Marlon kicked the door wide open and stormed inside the apartment.

A shrill scream entered my ears. I was stunned for a second at how high-pitched it sounded. That wasn't Faion. There was a woman in there.

I ordered my legs to follow Marlon. As soon as I got to the door, I found him with his gun fixed on Lily.

"My god, put that stupid gun away," I said.

Why the hell did he even need a gun? He could tear a professional wrestler apart with his bare hands in mere seconds.

"Lil, I'm so sorry," I said. The poor thing was shaking in my arms.

"What's happening? What is this?" Lily said.

Where do I begin?

"We thought someone had broken in."

"*We?*" She bent her face at Marlon, half-terrified, half-curious.

"Yeah... Lily, this is Marlon, my...um, bodyguard. Marlon, this is Lily."

I expected her to fall into stunned silence or maybe laugh in my face, not believing a word. Instead, she furrowed her brow as she took a closer look at the brutish wall of muscle and tattoos that was Marlon.

"Your bodyguard?" she said. "That's... hot."

"What? That's not hot. No, Lily. You had a gun in your face. It's traumatizing. You should be in shock."

"Uh huh," she said. "I am. It's kind of interesting."

That girl's libido, I swear.

I took a peek at the head of Cyrus's security, wondering how this girlie talk was affecting him. He didn't flinch. His eyes focused on the wall behind Lily and me as if we didn't exist.

"Anyway, I'm sorry for that," I said. "What are you doing here?"

"My place is being fumigated and Lucia is a bit much today. I needed a moment to myself. Thought you wouldn't mind."

"Of course, anytime."

"Sophie…" she said. "Why do you have a muscle statue with a gun in your living room? Is he doing more to your body than guarding it? I simply need to hear every detail immediately. And go slow on the good parts."

"It's a whole thing," I said. "Messy as it sounds."

"Okay, that's a good start. Is he the mysterious boyfriend I haven't met, or maybe a single employee of your phantom hook up? You told me it was getting serious. I didn't know it was *give-you-a-bodyguard* serious. I'm not sure that's healthy but this guy looks *really healthy*."

I turned to Marlon. "Okay, Marlon, do you mind giving us privacy?"

He took his sweet time thinking about it. Lily pinched my arm, failing to contain a chuckle. His serious demeanor was too much for her.

"I can't go far," he said. "This is not a secure location."

"How about just outside the door?"

We watched him lift his shirt and tuck the gun in a hidden holster. He nodded before walking out the door.

"Don't go far, Marlon," Lily said as she watched his behind. "We both need your protection. Me first though."

"I'm sure he heard that," I said. "You know if you were a man, you'd be cancelled right now."

"Shush, I'm in shock," she said.

I laughed. No one made me laugh like Lily.

"Alright, Collinsworth, let's hear it. Spill."

I took in a deep breath. "I'm getting married."

Her eyes became saucers. "Get the fuck out of here."

I really wish I could, Lil.

I shook my head. "I swear. Turns out, it's really serious."

"Wait, let me get my head around this. First there was Emmet, then Jonas, now this... does he actually have a name?"

"Maybe this is why nothing ever happened between me and Emmet, or Jonas. I was meant for Cyrus. That's his name. And the bodyguard thing... Cyrus owns several businesses, and one of them is a security firm, and sometimes he gets carried away with protecting his princess."

She listened closely, growing ever more restless. "That's kind of odd, giving you a bodyguard. A bit chauvinistic, too. He seems a bit more my type than yours. I never minded a little old world male overreach, but not you."

Ugh. She knows me too well.

"Right? It's all a big surprise to me, too. Completely out

of left field. And Marlon's not really my bodyguard, he's the head of the security firm and wanted to check out where I live."

Lily struggled to find words. That was a first. "It's all a little off…"

"Lily, I'm happy."

She took me in her arms. "Then that's all that matters."

I lingered in the embrace because lying to her of all people was quickly taking a toll on me.

"What else have you been hiding? Tell me everything. I missed you."

"I haven't been hiding."

"Then why haven't I seen this guy? Does he have a horse head or something?" She scrunched up her face. "You know what? We're having dinner tomorrow night, the three of us. It's settled. I won't take no for an answer. I'm going to see this BoJack with my own eyes. I'll see what's wrong with him that you have him locked away somewhere out of sight."

Her instincts are too good sometimes. It's eerie.

"His name is Cyrus, not BoJack, and there's absolutely nothing wrong with him," I said. "He has a normal human head."

Sometimes.

"Perfect," she said, "then there's no good reason for me not to meet him. I'll expect you both at 7 o'clock sharp."

"Fine," I said, "and I'll invite Emmet, too. He and Cyrus are old friends. Emmet actually introduced us."

I could only hope Emmet would accept the invitation. I didn't know how long I could maintain the charade without him.

Lily shook her head. "This is so messy."

Times a billion.

"I told you."

Marlon stepped inside. "There's someone here to see you."

"I'm popular today," I said, walking to the door.

Faion's head peeked in. "Is it safe? A lot of toxic female energy in here. Still recovering from the trauma of my last visit to Sophie's world."

Shoot, the whole Lily affair took so much out of me, I'd forgotten why I was there, to meet Faion.

Lily arched an eyebrow. "What an odd thing to say."

"That's Faion. Always with the jokes," I said. I grabbed Faion's collar and pulled him inside.

Faion stared at Lily, then Marlon, wondering why I had brought company to a private conversation. Another first. He couldn't find words.

"It's the prodigal son," Lily said. "And why haven't you answered a single text in like a week, Faion?"

"Blame Joey," Faion said, apologetic look on his face. "He took me on a surprise getaway."

"Uh huh. To the land without 5G?"

Bingo, but really, why isn't there 5G in the deep down?

"That's funny, but, no, Joey wanted this whole couple

bonding and healing and all that new age mumbo jumbo stuff."

Not believable, Faion, drop it.

"Whatever, you two are both in friendship jail," Lily said. "Lucia roped me into helping with her new project. She's opening a bakery. And don't think I'll forget about tomorrow, Soph. Me, you and Monsieur Horseman."

"A bakery?" I said. How many episodes of the Lucia saga had I missed?

"I can be a taste tester," Faion offered.

"No way," Lily said from outside. "You're in a timeout."

Marlon cleared his throat. "I've checked inside and outside, I see no water damage or repair of water damage."

"That will be all, Marlon," I said, echoing the way Cyrus talked.

Marlon closed the door, leaving me alone with Faion.

Faion tilted his head. "How did you just talk to Marlon? That sounded like a rich lady on the BBC."

"Cyrus is a terrible influence. Never mind all that. You've been in the Deep Down?"

He nodded. "I was visiting my Gran."

"How is Celia?"

"Like always. She steady. Listen, Luna, it's getting weird down deep. Seers and diviners have felt sealed time portals being breached."

"That's not good," I said.

Faion rolled his eyes. "Thank you, Miss Obvious. I'll relay

that message to my Divining Order, I'm sure they hadn't realized."

I rolled my eyes. "Stop being mean. I'm just impatient to know what happened last night."

"A time portal cut through the wards and materialized right inside the Encinitas gate. I wasn't there, but I heard the battle was brutal."

"Who did we have to fight?"

"Not who... what. Supernatural creatures of all kinds bursting through the portal, scent phantoms, polymorphs, arachnoids. Our elite mage and sorcerer forces had to be called in to fight them off."

"Those creatures have all been exiled long ago," I said to myself.

Faion nodded. "Not just that. They were extra. They had strong magic, Luna. Beyond strong. Horpheus himself had to bum-rush the gate to force them back into the portal. They sealed the gate, but no one trusts the seal anymore. It's under heavy guard, but little good that will do when the portal opens somewhere else as they are apt to do."

"It already has," I said. "Right here, in San Diego, by the Symphony Towers. Luckily it was closed quickly before anything happened, but it's not a good sign. Tell Celia. Horpheus must be informed. I have a very bad feeling about this, Faion."

"Gran said you best stay away."

Celia was right. My true essence needed to stay hidden.

I took my friend's hand. "The time is coming, Faion. Soon. I feel it. A time when we'll no longer have the luxury of choice."

Chapter 6

DESPITE THE UNEXPECTED SUMMER rain, the line outside Cheesecake Factory was growing longer. Lucky for us, Cyrus had made a last-minute reservation as soon as I told him about the dinner.

At the lobby, Lily and I stared at the scrumptious, mouthwatering cheesecakes in the display case. We did this every time we went there.

Lily had a new haircut, a short bob with auburn highlights. It somehow made her face even cuter. She wore a sleeveless, midnight-blue duchesse and organza dress that was not her usual casual chic style but looked perfect on her anyway. That night she literally glowed.

I straightened my yellow halter dress, the one with sunflowers, that reached my knees and cost me thirty-eight dollars on sale from fifty.

Thankfully, Emmet found someone to take over his shift

at the hospital. He had agreed to dinner after I begged, then threatened and, finally, said please many times in a row. Every woman has that trick in her tool kit.

"We were not properly introduced," Cyrus told Lily, offering his hand. He held only Lily's fingers and gently like an eighteenth-century gentleman. "Cyrus McDonnell," he said. "It's a pleasure."

I reluctantly accepted that he was visually appealing to most women. Not hot like Winter, but he had luscious brown hair and sun-kissed bronze skin that had a sexy, rugged effect when contrasted with his white linen shirt.

Lily's eyes hid none of her thoughts. If we were on a boat, she might push me over the side. "Lily Herrero," she said.

Did she just lick her lips?

I pulled her down on the bench next to me in the waiting area. I couldn't help but notice the sparkle in her eyes. Cyrus and Emmet remained standing and began a conversation among themselves.

Lily leaned over to me. "Is he a vampire? Those eyes."

Wrong Twilight guy, Lily.

"More than you know," I said.

"I knew it. He has that *born long ago* vibe."

"Well, his charm does get old fast."

Lily's eyes widened. "Are you sure you like this guy? Because that was kind of messed up."

I laughed. "No, Lil, I just really love messing with him. He does the same to me. That's our flirt game."

"That's really hot," she said. "I want that."

I hate lying to her.

She pointed at the white chocolate raspberry truffle cheesecake in the window. "Holy hell, look at that," she said for all to hear. "Just reading its name makes your mouth water."

"Hard to tell if it was an angel or a devil who made that," I said.

"Women look at cake like men look at women," Cyrus said. "It's more than a little obscene."

The server beckoned us just in time.

Emmet grinned at Lily. "Cyrus says things like that. Don't worry, he'll grow on you."

I was grateful Lily refrained from voicing any of the many double entendre lines that must have been flooding her head.

Lily ended up sitting next to Emmet and across from me. As I opened the menu, she winked at me happily.

"What are you having?" I asked Lily.

"I already told the guy when he sat us. Greek olives with feta cheese to start with," she said before she turned her attention to Cyrus. "It's so nice to finally meet you. Sophie has been so frugal with information, keeping you all to herself."

"I'm afraid I am not much more than a businessman. It's not Sophie's fault. Signing paychecks is not as exciting as scoring tickets to Coachella or throwing touchdowns for the Aztecs. A serious man is not the type of man who travels well through secondhand stories."

"Hmm, that's a bit humble, a bit gracious and even a bit smooth. And I think you know that. I'm still not quite seeing this," Lily said.

"Oh, and what *are* you seeing?" Cyrus said, perhaps losing patience.

"Wouldn't you like to know?" she said.

Cyrus feigned amusement.

She batted her eyelashes. "Hey, big boy, let's get one thing straight. If you're using all that experience and slick talking insincerely with my innocent little friend here, you're going to get cut."

Now that it happened, I realized I should have always known it was going to happen. She was my best friend. She knew when something was not good for me even before I did. And so, Lily threatened the Higher Alpha of the San Diego pack, a dude that turned into a huge black panther just so he can happily partake in his favorite endeavor, ripping flesh from bone with his teeth.

"Really?" Cyrus said, actually amused this time.

Was he flirting with her? He better not be or I'd be the one cutting him.

"Big time," Lily said, eyeing the menu.

I slapped her hand. "Lily's as subtle as a sledgehammer."

Cyrus retrieved my hand and placed it on his thigh. He winked to let me know he had me right where he wanted and there was nothing I could do about it. "You know, Lily, I like your show of loyalty, but it goes both ways. If you should do anything to put my girl in danger, you're going to have to answer to me."

Lily tilted her neck and widened her eyes. "I answer to no man. Neither does she. I suggest you learn that before you really piss her off."

"I've seen her temper," Cyrus said. "It brings the loveliest color to her cheeks. I discover something new and fantastic about her every day."

Lily locked her eyes on mine. "He's cute, but you're going to need to train him," she said before returning to the menu.

"How does it feel?" Emmet said. "They're pulling on your arms like you're a wishbone."

"It's okay, I'm not going to break," I said. "They're both stubborn, which means they have to lock horns a little. It's entertainment."

The waiter arrived with the olives and cheese Lily had ordered. She clapped her hands enthusiastically at the sight. She took some on her plate then passed the rest on to me. I stabbed an olive and held it under my nose.

"Greek olives," I said. "So good."

Lily put an olive in Emmet's mouth with her fingers.

Cyrus kicked him under the table. "Speaking of Greece, Emmet, aren't you flying there next year?"

That piqued Lily's interest. "Greece?" she said. "Really?"

Emmet seemed caught off guard. "Ah, yeah," he said. "In the spring."

Something told me this was Cyrus's idea. But why?

"A new adventure?" I asked.

"I'm hoping to talk to doctors there who are doing break-through research in the sports medicine field."

"It's his specialty," Cyrus clarified.

"My specialty is traveling," Lily said, leaning on Emmet, then wrapping her arm around him. "Please, Emmet, I won't bother your research. In fact, I'll cook and type your notes." She turned to me. "Maybe I'll take a Greek lover or a fun-loving Turk or, who knows, a roaming Sudanese."

"A *roaming Sudanese*," Emmet said, charmed It was clear that the good doctor had never come across anyone quite like Lily.

"She's a collector," I said, but no one found my joke charming.

"Yeah," Emmet said, blushing. "The more the merrier."

Greece thought it had gone through a rough patch recently, wait until Lily landed on their shores. Better guard your sons and your liquor cabinets.

"Let's go," Lily said, looking at me.

"Huh?"

"Where's your mind off to? The restroom."

I followed her obediently. As soon as we were out of earshot of the guys, she took my arm. "I take back what I said. Cyrus is as delicious as he's smug, and apparently loaded," she said. "I can see why he swept you off your feet."

My cheeks heated. Pretending to be in love with Cyrus McDonnell in front of my best friend of all people felt like a kick in the stomach.

Lily posed in front of the big mirror to pull her bra up and fix her hair.

"Actually, I don't know which of them is better looking," she said as I pulled my lipstick out of my purse.

I stared at my image in the mirror, trying to gage if she was serious. "Does that mean you'd be interested in Emmet?"

She shook her head. "Emmet? He's cool and hot but—"

"But what?"

Lily's eyes focused on me. "I would never want to date your ex-boyfriend. That would just be awkward, like kissing my cousin."

"For the hundredth time, there was nothing serious between us. We had a couple of dates, that's it."

"Still," she said, grabbing my arm. "C'mon, let's get back before Cyrus starts to worry. That dude has it bad for you. Did you hear him threaten me? That was yummy."

"I think you started it."

"Shut," Lily said. "I did no such thing."

Walking back to our table we witnessed a heated exchange between Cyrus and Emmet.

Lily frowned. "Your boyfriend's a whole mood."

"WHAT WERE YOU AND Emmet arguing about?" I asked Cyrus as we walked to his red Lexus. Five shadows trailed behind us at a distance—shifter security.

"Trivial stuff. Yellow is your color, by the way," he said.

Yellow? Ah, my dress. Right. What an ass kisser. "Thanks, but I'm a brunette. Yellow can't possibly be my color."

"Can't you take a compliment? You don't have to be a hard ass all the time. All I'm trying to say, Sophie, is that you look stunning tonight."

"You're too transparent," I said, walking past him, hoping he'd stop staring at me like I was his next meal. "I hope you'll feel that way about the dress I'm wearing at the wedding because it's going to be black."

"You'd look good in a potato sack."

Dude, what I wouldn't give to smack him upside the head. He must think there's no woman on the planet who won't fall for his tired lines. All part of his master plan to throw me off.

"Really?" I said. "The plastic kind or the old burlap ones?"

"Oh, yeah, definitely plastic," he said with delight.

"Okay, great," I said. "I'm fake marrying Dexter. Just my luck."

He grinned and stared at me. "I'm not all that bad."

"You're worse, but I don't care. What I want to know is why you're sending Emmet away."

"I'm doing what?"

"It couldn't be more obvious."

"It could be more obvious," he said. "Perhaps if it was true."

"You're impossible," I said.

"And yet here I am. Behold. The impossible come to life."

This dude.

"I'm surprised you don't tip over with that ego," I said.

"You're right. My words are not enough. What did Lily think of your soon-to-be-husband?"

"Lily? Really? Let me recall. She said you're spectacularly unattractive, have unmatched arrogance and, oh yeah, you smell funny."

He quickly circled the car to get the door for me. "I smell funny?"

"You smell fine," I said. "Get a clue. I obviously made that up, but I've lost my patience, Cyrus. I'm not getting in the car unless I hear your plans for Emmet."

He stared at me. "There's a new wolf pack forming in southern Europe. They asked for our help against some older local pack mafia. I want Emmet in charge of the transition process."

It made no sense. "Emmet wasn't even in your pack until recently."

"Until you almost got him killed," he corrected me.

I suppressed an urge to blast him with an energy bolt. "Why him?"

"Because he's capable, he's intelligent and he can rapidly climb the hierarchy ladder—and because he's vulnerable here."

"Vulnerable how?"

He arched an eyebrow.

"You mean because of me?"

"Yes. I want him as far away from you as possible."

"You're a fucking lunatic."

"He'd run right back to you if you waved your little pinky at him, and you know it. And, maybe, you even like it."

I would kill him. I'd wait for the right moment and... *bam!* "Emmet and I have an understanding. We've moved on. He's not a little boy and he definitely doesn't need you or me or anybody else to tell him what he should feel."

"It's not his feelings I'm worried about," Cyrus said. "It's the fact you will never return them. Instead, you'll keep him friend-zoned for life, right under your thumb."

I couldn't believe my ears. "You arrogant prick. Just when you seem a tiny bit human, and I start to give you the benefit of the doubt and think that maybe we can have a real talk about how Darius is using us both... that's when you go ahead and prove you're the most controlling, mega dick on the planet."

He didn't miss a beat. "I didn't think you noticed."

"Oh my god. You're not just an asshole, you're delusional. If I didn't know better, I'd say you're jealous."

"Good thing you always know better, because I'd never be the puppet of a newborn witch like Emmet has become. I'd end my own life first."

"You know what? Screw this. Marlon's driving me home."

I walked straight over to the five shadows. "Marlon, please drive me to that idiot's giant doghouse prison."

"This way," he said.

"No offense," I said, realizing my insensitivity.

I was seething—my hands tingled with energy overload. There was no damn way I would ever allow Cyrus McDonnell to exile Emmet just to give his already swelling ego yet another boost.

Chapter 7

WHEN IT RAINS, IT pours. Now Lucia wanted to meet Cyrus, she expected Gram to stay at her house the week of the wedding so they could bond, and she also insisted on baking my wedding cake.

My mist rider energy reacted to my stress and boiled, eager to wipe out the entire pack compound, Cyrus and Darius included as a sweetener—except then, the Ten Thousand Immortals who guarded Winter would chop him to pieces and incinerate his heart.

I called Kirsi to vent before I lost my mind.

"*Good timing,*" Kirsi said. "*I received another message.*"

"On your fridge?"

"*No, in my mailbox. Let me read it to you.*"

I steeled myself for even worse news.

"*Search the Ephemera Almanacs for the financial institu-tion.*"

"I have no idea what that means."

"The Ephemera Almanacs are the Seventh's highly classified archives of banned data. It's basically impossible to access, but as Guard of the Council Seal, I may be able to pull it off."

"Not if Düsternis has anything to say about it."

"He's away. No one knows where. It's the perfect opportunity for me to quietly enter the magistrate courts and start digging."

This was exactly why Kirsi had not broken her ties with the council. Her title and clout meant access and sometimes access was everything.

"Did you finish the journal?"

"Yeah. There was nothing new. They must have made it very clear to Susan what would happen if she opened her mouth. There is not one name or specific detail in the journal that might be connected to the tragedy to come."

"Kirsi, be careful."

"Careful is not what I do."

As soon as we hung up, I hurried off to search for Marlon. I found him in the vast open lobby that had been repurposed into security offices.

His eyes were puffy, and a tired yawn escaped his mouth the moment he saw me approaching. He had the look of a man who was up late last night gambling or fighting or chasing women. His three favorite vices.

"I need to go to town," I told him. "I'll be discreet, I'll sneak out. If anyone asks, you didn't see a thing. Tell them I must have used magic or whatever pops into your head."

Let's be honest, not much popped into his head. He'd blame it on magic.

"Same curse, different day," he said, heading for the coffee machine.

"Dude, I'm going to lose you anyway, don't waste your time."

He spat coffee out of the side of his mouth. "Fucking Joan of Arc. I don't know why the Higher Alpha doesn't discipline you properly."

Try to be nice to some people...

Cyrus had told me many times the respect of a shapeshifter is hard earned and quickly lost.

I let energy spark in my eyes as I fixed Marlon in my gaze. "You're forgetting yourself, wolf. Soon I'll be second-in-command around here. That means I can discipline you. Take my word, you don't want me for an enemy."

Magic thrust from my fingertips, forming a small bolt of energy that hung in the air between us.

Marlon flared his nostrils. "I was out of line. Forgive me."

"Forgiven. Just don't make it a habit and we're cool."

"Listen, I'm going to grab a few winks," he said, spilling the rest of his coffee in the sink. "I might or might not turn off the security cameras on the west gate to update the software."

I headed to the west gate through a long corridor. I started to enjoy each step as I was about to leave the property unfollowed for the first time.

"Sophie."

Fucking hell.

I turned back. Cyrus waved me over.

"Been looking for you," he said. "The way we left things last night... It wasn't cool. I was being a prick and I want to make it up to you."

"The apology is more than enough. There's nothing to make up."

"I insist," he said. "Am I interrupting you from something?"

"No, just getting some fresh air."

His eyebrows came together. "Through the west gate? It leads straight to the storage facilities."

"Does it?"

"Yeah, it's not the best place for a stroll."

"Trying to find something new in this prison maze," I said.

"Perfect, then come with me. I have a real surprise."

"Why do I have a hundred alarms going off inside me?"

"Fuck that," he said. "You're going to like this."

I followed him back through the atrium and all the way to his large private parking garage that could fit a dozen vehicles.

Cyrus walked up to a brand-new burnt orange sedan. He stroked the car hood like it was a newborn puppy. "That's a Lexus LS and that's a custom paint job. Cadmium Orange. Look at that sick soul glow."

"You're really into Lexus cars," I said.

"I am, but we also have a deal in place with a local dealership. They are friends of the pack and give us healthy discounts."

"Hooray for you," I said, losing interest.

He opened his hand to produce a key fob. "Hooray for you, too."

I stared at him. "Seriously? Are you trying to bribe me with a car?"

Cyrus grinned. "Consider it a wedding present. No bride of mine will be left on foot or driving a subpar ride. It would reflect poorly on me."

Does he really think he has a stellar reputation?

"And you realize what cars are used for, right?" I said. "You're cool with me just driving anywhere anytime I get the urge?"

"Of course. It's yours. Our alliance serves a very specific purpose, Sophie, but you're not my prisoner. Keep your end of the bargain, and you can live your life however you see fit."

Wow, he was laying it on a little too thick.

"No," I said, "I'm not buying it. The only reason you'd give me a car is because you've installed a dozen tracking systems, so you'll know where I am at all times. It will make shadowing me easier, right? Your security team failed you, so you came up with the car idea to control and manipulate me."

"It's just a car. It has GPS, of course, but you could

obviously park and get in a friend's car at any point. The GPS is there in case you disappear. It would give us a starting point. There are ancient entities who wish you harm. Don't lose sight of the big picture. The car, it's yours. It's fucking cool. You can take her out for a spin right now. Or not. That's your choice."

"Free will has been out the window since I first laid eyes on you."

He sighed. "Do you know how you subdue a big predator cat? You simply stare into their eyes, unblinking, and you don't turn away. You swallow your fear and doubts, and you persist. That's how animal tamers dominate tigers and train them to perform tricks."

"Apt since you're running a circus."

He chuckled. "I've had grizzly-bear and buffalo shifters cower into a corner shivering when I stared them down. Do you know what I see when I stare into your eyes? You're indomitable. You're brimming with power. I can feel you holding back, probably been that way every day of your life. I respect that. It's a sign of real strength. I know you can't be controlled."

"Then tell Darius you changed your mind about the wedding," I said. "Me being here at the compound just makes all of you less safe."

"We can handle ourselves but, believe it or not, moving out of the compound would make matters worse for you."

"Right, this is all for my benefit. You're all talk, Cyrus.

You're a power-hungry pack alpha with an agenda. This is about the pack, about what benefits your little shifter cult most."

"That's my charge, I don't deny it. I'm responsible for the wellbeing of hundreds of lives. I don't take it lightly. And I've taken on the responsibility for yours as well."

"Give me the key," I said.

He hesitated.

"Go on, give me my key, then. I don't have to switch cars. I'll neutralize the GPS trackers with an energy shield. One of the many things any lunar witch can conjure in a snap."

He threw the key fob up. To show off, I used an energy field to slow it down and land it on my palm as gently as a feather.

I stepped into the car and locked the door. I slid the window down to look up at Cyrus. "The car changes nothing, but thanks."

Twenty minutes later, I pulled up to the coffee shop. I enjoyed the clicking sound when I hit the lock button while walking to the front door.

Maura beamed when she saw me. "Sophie, you back to work a shift?"

I gave her a hug. "Hell, no. It's great to see you, Maura."

"Likewise, my little chickadee. Big Rob will be bummed he missed you. He's off today, but he gets puppy dog eyes every time your name comes up."

"That's sweet, but no worries, I'm sticking around for a

while," I said. "There'll be plenty of opportunities to see him."

I sat in a happy daze by the window with my vanilla latte. I needed a moment to decompress. Cyrus was ramping up his game. The car, the more I thought about it, was a plot point in a slow-moving seduction plan. He wanted to groom me until I wanted a real marriage, or at least until I trusted him. He sensed the power in me? I'm sure he did, and he wanted to use my power for his own designs. He knew it wasn't going to work. So, why did he insist on giving it his best shot anyway? That worried me.

"Double espresso, brown sugar."

I knew that earthly baritone voice and its notable accent.

Milan Visser handed his credit card to Maura at the counter. He turned, expecting my eyes on him. He raised a finger in greeting. Maura returned his credit card. He thanked her in a way that made her giggle.

He seemed less like a lawyer and more like an international man of intrigue. He filled the room with his powerful physicality, gallant manners and his red cedar and mint cologne.

"Miss Collinsworth, what good fortune to see you again."

"Mr. Visser, is it?"

He bowed. "Indeed. You remembered. I wonder, might you have the item we discussed in your possession?"

"I do."

"And did it help you find what you were looking for?"

"That's a whole thing," I said, "and I'd rather not discuss it."

"Of course, that's wise. Very good, let me leave you to your latte."

He turned away but changed his mind. He stepped back to face me, fist over his mouth.

"Yes?" I said.

"There's one thing you should know."

The way he said that gave me pause. "Only one?"

He brushed his hair back with his fingers. "I share this in strict confidence. Our mutual acquaintance said something that I found quite... how shall I say? *Implausible.*" He hesitated. "He mentioned that many decades later, his dying father had encountered the person who had enlisted his wife's assistance on the night she died."

"And?"

"A curious thing, he said they hadn't changed a bit. No wrinkles, no slouching, no crow's feet by the eyes. It's as if time had not laid a single hand on this person. Quite an astonishing claim, don't you think?"

I sat very still, trying to come up with an appropriate response.

"I suppose he was very old when he claims to have seen the person," Milan Visser continued. "Hardly eyes to be trusted."

"Then why are you telling me?"

"Because it was quite unusual. And, really, you should take everything this family tells you with a grain of salt. It's unprofessional of me to cast my opinion, but you seem like someone who deserves a break. In all good conscience, I had to mention that and warn you." He spun his index finger over his temple. "Sometimes, I think they're not altogether there."

"Alright, thank you, Mr. Visser. I'll surely keep it in mind."

"You have my card."

I watched Milan Visser walk out the door. He held his coffee like a gentleman from European literature. First, he showed up at my apartment, then at my old workplace. It was all too convenient, entirely too neat. He had the air of someone who had never once been fooled.

Was he the harbinger of doom, or was he the doom itself?

Chapter 8

I CLUTCHED ONTO WINTER'S enchanted Nordic sword in the dark. I repeated that ritual every night, hoping against hope that the blade would flicker, and thus give me proof that Winter had regained consciousness. The sword had strong magic and could recognize Winter's etheric essence as it rippled through space and time. Even the faintest glow of the blade would mean some ember of Winter's energy core still burned.

I pricked my finger with the tip of the blade. A warm drop of blood trickled down my palm. I had seconds to lick it up before the wound healed. My blood bonded me to Chaos and our father, Horror. They could both communicate with me telepathically. If I dropped my shields, I had no doubt they'd be dropping DMs through every pathway in my mind.

That sort of invasion terrified me. I had to learn my

blood's magic and understand its power if I was ever to control the connective blood pathway myself—someday, I might even get strong enough to access Horror's blood language itself.

It suddenly grew hot in my room at the Keep. A blue light flickered outside the window. A wave of magic washed through me like an icy stream. I gripped the sword and jumped to my feet. Nothing stirred, just my breath and my glowing hand.

A whooshing sound ricocheted off the walls all around me. Chaos materialized in tendrils of blue smoke, his familiar impish grin, dark coal eyes and shining black hair glistening midnight-blue within the fading smoke.

"Now you see me, now you don't," he said and vanished. *What an idiot.*

A second later, he reappeared. The smoke dispersed into sparkling particles and then, just as quickly, faded away.

"That wasn't a bit," he said. "I just forgot my shake."

He gripped a Jimmy Dean's cup in his hand, lining the straw up to his mouth. When he started to suck, he made more gurgling straw noise than any teenager could ever produce.

I punched his biceps with the hilt of the sword. "You finally decided to show your face, huh? I could have used your help, you silly fool."

He rubbed his biceps, then set down his shake to snatch up my Mars bar from the dresser.

"I'm not Sophie's little helper. You have enough of those. I'm here because despite all my fucking warnings and the colossal effort I put into bringing the damn message home, you've been consorting with daddy dearest."

Huh?

"No, I haven't. Your antennae must be busted."

He licked chocolate from his lips. "First rule of Shadow Club: never lie to a Shadow if you still have a conscience. Lying is not one of your powers, little lamb. You talked to Horror and that recklessness won't fly with the Lord of the Black Demon Hounds."

"Dude, seriously, that's paranoid nonsense you're spitting."

He circled me, sniffing at the air around me. "You walked next to him. You talked to him. Yes, yes, you did. Our connective pathway oozes with his dark power. You let him in, Luna, and you didn't even hesitate."

I raised the sword in front of his chest to stop him from circling me. I hated when men did that. "Okay, cards on the table," I said. "He's been visiting my head and talking to me through the blood pathway. I allowed it, but I'm staying alert in case he lets his guard down just enough for me to glimpse into his deranged mind and figure out his next move."

Chaos laughed heartily. "Bless your heart, cupcake. In the magic department, he's a million miles out of your league. Well, in *every* department, but it's cute you think you can catch him off guard and insanely moronic. You're lucky

I double sealed this room, or he'd be in your head right now, pulling at your kitty strings. And no, I wasn't talking about telepathic connection. You've been in the same physical space as that bastard."

I stared at him. "Wouldn't I sense that? If he was near?"

"Don't know, would you? Maybe you're blind to it."

"How? Does he use time portals like you to surface behind me when I'm taking a walk? Has he been following me? Is he invisible?"

"Ay, my moon-brained sister is slow on the uptake. Have you been listening? You talked to him. You even touched him."

Touched him? I racked my brain for encounters with strangers I'd somehow touched and I came up empty. Could it be a waiter? A hair salon stylist? Maybe we had bumped into each other?

"Well, show me what he looks like."

"Sure, let me just pull up his Instagram. Horror has many faces, sister, he can be any age, he can be frail or robust. Who do you think gave Cerber his ability to face-change?"

Of course, Horror was the ultimate Face Changer. No doubt next time he made an appearance inside my head, he'd offer to pass that nifty trick on to me as well. *Yikes.* He was still in the luring phase and would try enticing me with honey instead of making threats.

Who could he be? A grocer? A mail carrier? A shifter? Any shifter at the compound? Or maybe... *No, no fucking way!*

Unless... no, it didn't make sense... all that polish, all that refinement...

I rummaged through my purse for Milan Visser's business card. If his credentials held up to scrutiny, I'd take him off the suspect list.

I dialed the number on the card. The line rang once, then went dead. I googled the law firm *Visser, Michaels and Landon*. No such firm in San Diego. No such firm anywhere. The arrogant jerk didn't even try. He wanted me to know what he'd done. That's why he gave me the card in the first place.

Nausea welled up to my throat. I tossed the phone on the bed with a growl, then picked it up quick to make sure I hadn't fried it. My phones had a nasty habit of blowing up on me.

"What do you have against your phone?" Chaos said.

I handed him the card. "This man said he was a lawyer."

Chaos bent over, slapped his knees and huffed happily.

"Fuck you. What? How would I know?"

I waited for him to stop cackling. It took a while.

He tried to compose himself. "Milan is his absolute favorite alias. He often used it to roam the basic world incognito. Been a long while. *Milan*, shit. That's him. That most definitely is him."

The world unraveled around me. My hateful, megalomaniac father, one of the very first Eternals, who dipped his magic so deep into the darkness it became catastrophic, managed to glide through my front door, sit on my couch and spin a completely bullshit story. He watched as I lapped it all up. When we shook hands, the bastard had held on as long as he could to make sure the contact would register with Chaos's sensors.

Of course, Chaos had sensed him. Horror wanted it that way.

Chaos paced the room. "The concern here isn't that he made contact, but that you didn't sense him. He's unmatched at cloaking his essence, but with one who carries his blood, it shouldn't be possible. Which means you are still grossly untrained and completely open to manipulation."

"If that's all true, where were you, brother?" I said. "You knew Horror had learned of my existence."

"Oy, you want to blame someone, blame your heart-struck mentor. It was his job to prepare you, and what did he do? Develop feelings like a fucking schoolboy human. Such an embarrassment to all Shadow kind."

Chaos was not all wrong. I should have sensed *something*. I should have at least known Milan Visser was not basic. My etheric intuition had never failed so spectacularly before.

He studied me. "Are you sure you felt nothing?"

"I don't think... no, wait, his ring did give me some strange vibes when I shook his hand."

"What kind of ring?"

"A signet ring with red lettering."

His face went pale. "That's the Thespian ring. If Horror

has it, that means he waltzed through the Eternal Halls undetected, breached the vault that stored all his magic artifacts and absorbed knowledge of the modern world."

"How could he do that?"

"Some new magic unknown to our world," he said.

Well, isn't that peachy?

"What's so special about the Thespian ring?"

"When he wears the ring, he becomes mortal," Chaos explained. "Don't get excited, cupcake, it doesn't mean he can be killed, but his molecular structure alters and weakens his aura and his energy core. It mimics a *basic* state. He could pick a new face and live in the basic world for centuries and none would be the wiser, not even the Eternals."

If he could fool Eternals, no wonder he pulled a fast one on me. "I don't think he plans to disappear in the world of mortals. He came to me because he wants something. He knew you'd be here now to tip me off. That's why he let you sense our contact."

Chaos looked about the room as if for the first time. "What is this ghastly lodging? Have you been locked in a dog pound?"

Right, he didn't know. He had left before Darius double-crossed me.

I unloaded. I gave him a full account of the events: how Darius was behind Chaos's capture by Düsternis, how he had kidnapped Winter and Arsha, how he had forced me to stay in the pack compound and marry Cyrus to ensure

Winter and Arsha's safety.

He listened patiently until I was done and then he lost it. He kicked my desk chair and sent it flying across the room. His eyes blistered with rage. A dark aura rose and flared about him like a sinister cloak. "That smarmy d-bag, that ancient piece of excrement. I warned you. I told you he'd claim you. I'm taking you out of here. A spider hole in the desert would be better than this life-sucking animal graveyard."

Sadness overtook every cell in my body. "If I don't do as Darius says, Winter dies. Even you can't want that."

His eyes ignited with pure hatred. "Let me deal with Darius. I'll find out where he keeps your frosty fanboy. If that mad hatter thinks he can hide from the third-eye vision, he's an even bigger fool than I thought. Continue as you are... don't eliminate the childish behavior or whining. Don't let anyone think that anything has changed."

I miss being an only child.

"I'll bolster my shields to keep Horror out of my head," I said.

"Listen when I speak. You... can't... change... ONE THING! Blocking psycho Pop from your mind will only make him suspicious. He'll try to reach you in other ways. Trust me, lesser sibling, you don't want an unstable Horror stalking you. There's nothing that escapes the watchful eye of the Great Master of whatever they call him. There's no telling how much of his power he has reclaimed. Better play it smart, eh? Let him inside your head, yes, but guard your knowledge of me."

"How do I do that?"

Chaos chortled. "You are a mist rider, figure it out. Practice, then learn what you can from the old bastard. If he offers you some of his magic tricks, accept them. You'll need all the weapons you can get." He stopped, a new idea forming in his head. "Tell me, what did he look like?"

"Tall, strawberry blond hair, high cheekbones, green eyes, refined manners, in short, the opposite of you."

Chaos was flabbergasted. "The bloody numbskull used his real face. Very few have ever seen it. Luna, he needs something he thinks only you can give him. He'll stop at nothing to win you over. Stay vigilant while I'm gone."

That was the real Horror? Comprehending that was more disturbing than if he had lizard eyes and a forked tail.

"How can that be him? He looked quite normal, polished, a man of fine manners, elegance and grace," I said. "How does he remain that refined after centuries in isolation? He even used a tablet like he was a sixteen-year-old gamer, like he was born with one in his hands. A tablet, Chaos. How has he remained so in sync with the times?"

He picked up a small perfume bottle and sniffed it. I snatched it away.

"Horror's a fast learner. He absorbs information like you take a breath." He hesitated. "Your mother stayed with him in his confinement, but she was allowed to return to the world four times a year for month-long visits. She must have kept him informed. He saw the world through her eyes."

Chaos would never willingly bring up my mother. Since I told him I knew we were half-siblings, he preferred to act like she didn't exist. Up to this moment, I hadn't fully grasped how hard it was for him to lose the woman he loved to his father, the very same woman who gave birth to me. I really wanted details on how it all went down, but I knew that story was still an open wound to Chaos.

"Is my mother Immortal then?" I said. "An Eternal?"

He sighed. "It changes nothing."

Holy shit... she is an Eternal!

"Daft witch, I can see the idea forming behind your doe eyes, rid that from the echo chamber of your puny head. She would never betray you to Horror. She'd guard your misty secrets with her life. That was the very reason she gave you up... I bet one of so few years hadn't even figured that out. She did that because she loved you and it tore her apart."

"Well... why did she stay with him, Chaos? She knew what Horror was capable of, she knew he would see me as a threat. You said it yourself, she tried to keep me away from him and yet, when she had the chance, when he was trapped in exile, when he couldn't stop her... she stayed."

Chaos engaged me with his intense eyes. "She knew to never underestimate him, nor should we. To destroy Horror, it will take us both, using his very own magic against him, and he knows it. Every breath we take is an alarm bell in his core. He won't let us grow strong enough. He won't let us live that long. Because of that certainty, we need as much help as we can find. We need that fool of yours, your feeble champion, Winter. And so, I must find him post-haste."

It would take Winter years to come out of his restorative mode, but if we could manage to free him from Darius's clutches, we could get to work on saving the rest of the world from Horror before he outgrew defeat.

I hugged Chaos. His arms went limp. I finally found a weapon to subdue him, my poor unloved brother. "We'll do it together."

"We can do nothing unless you release me," he said.

I let him out of my embrace. "It's just a hug, it's not Alcatraz."

Chapter 9

I FOUND MYSELF GLANCING up at everyone who walked into the coffee shop. My orange cranberry scone had been picked at until reduced to a pile of crumbs on my plate, very little of which ended up in my mouth.

Sitting in a dimly lit corner, I was convinced that every strange face threw shade my way, as if they knew I had dropped my shields on purpose, hoping to lure the foulest of necromancers to the coffee shop one more time.

I had been there an hour. Big Rob threw concerned glances at me from the counter. I opened my book and pretended to read. I started to think Horror had seen through my ill-conceived plan and wouldn't show up.

The bell above the door jingled. A tall man stepped in. Even though I couldn't see his face from where I sat, I knew it was him.

The air buzzed with electricity. How had I not felt this

the last time? His blood called to my veins like a potent hallucinogen.

A dull pang rose in my stomach. His true face still did not fit my idea of him, and it disturbed me. The entire coffee shop seemed to watch as he floated to me through the unnerving quiet.

I dismissed a weird sense of familiarity. Despite the genetics, it was not possible I had any shared traits with that Methuselah of a man.

A tinge of confusion overtook me as he filled up my frame of vision. The closer he got, the less certain I was about the wisdom of my plan. I intended to throw him off his game, but he had thrown me off mine already.

I looked away, but you didn't need to look at him to see him. Horror's essence lingered in the ether and infected all senses. I'd never felt such presence in my life. It was haunting, eviscerating, staggering.

I need to pull myself together.

The man who went by Milan Visser in the basic world stood before me, wearing cool black slacks and a slightly snug polo shirt.

His eyes were an unforgettable mix of blue and green, like some magic crystal from the planet Krypton.

Let's hope I'm not Supergirl.

"Sophie Collinsworth," he said with a deep, resonant voice that brought me back to reality.

"Mr. Visser, I see you've become a regular."

"I have some business in the area," he said, offering me his right hand.

I shook his hand and recoiled at the touch of the icy cold Thespian ring. Even his tanned hand with its long fingers and well-groomed nails oozed with a sneakily vicious aura.

I'm staring at his hand now. He must think I'm a dimwit.

"What a coincidence, me too," I said as I took my hand back.

His fathomless green ocean eyes narrowed as his hand returned to a pants pocket. "Do you mind if I sit?"

Yes, I do mind.

"Please, do."

He frowned at the mess on my plate. "Playing with your food?"

"What? No. Yeah, my eyes were bigger than my stomach. You know, it's lucky we ran into each other. I was going to call."

He sat back. "You have more questions?"

"It's that I've hit a roadblock," I said, stalling. "Perhaps Professor Rigby could help, yes. A couple more questions. Do you think you could use your influence on my behalf?"

He inhaled sharply. "My client made it quite clear he is done speaking on the matter."

Your client, huh? You duplicitous bastard.

"Maybe you know something," I suggested.

"Try me. Maybe I do."

"You mentioned Susan Rigby's friend, the one who hadn't aged."

He nodded.

"I found a passage in the journal that gave me pause. Susan wrote that the person who blackmailed her was not mortal. She describes it without any fuss and with clear detail, it almost sounds true."

He pursed his lips. "Santa Claus is described with even more detail by many people. Even sane people. It almost sounds true."

"She has an entry where she says the immortal slashed their own wrist and the wound healed within seconds. Why would she write something like that in her own diary if it weren't true?"

He considered the question. "You prefer it real?"

"I do."

"Susan Rigby was a disturbed woman. She had tried to take her own life on two occasions. One time by slashing her wrists."

I exhaled. "Oh, I see. Thanks for keeping it real."

Though he most certainly has made that up.

When he smiled, his charm was on high beam. "Of course."

"I have to figure out my next step," I said. "Have you ever thought about immortality? Wouldn't the isolation and loneliness of it be unbearable? Makes you think, doesn't it?"

He ran his fingers through his hair. "Interesting. That is

an entertaining contemplation. I think if you lived too long, you would lose your patience first, and then you might slip little by little away from the safe hold of moral constructs." He smiled. "That way lies madness."

"Yes, Mr. Visser. I agree totally. At some point boredom would be so overwhelming, the immortal would turn against the very things that once gave their life meaning and purpose."

The sparkle in his eyes turned green and blue all at once. The very same green hue found in my eyes.

"Such thoughts will corrupt the most durable minds, Miss Collinsworth. We are all eternal, however, for the particles that have made us are the very same as the ones that began the universe."

He stared at me with the swagger of someone who has always been in control and has never held a single doubt. My eyes dropped from his gaze.

Milan Visser left before I realized he had even stood. I watched him walk out, hands in pockets, with his long, loping strides.

I picked up my decimated scone and waved to Rob. I felt empty. Sitting in the presence of Horror sucked away all the vitality of one's soul.

In the parking lot I walked in a daze when Horror's voice boomed to life in my head. It felt like an army of ants walking across my brain pan.

"Daughter, the answers you seek... I have them."

It was excruciating to not let him read every hidden memory, every secret conversation, every dream and every moment with Chaos.

I gritted my teeth. "What are you even saying?"

"Your withering mentor," his voice said, "he fathered a son, a son who was murdered before his immortality could blossom. Do you want to know who killed the child, flower?"

It took all I had not to throw up. "Was it you?"

"It's always the one who stands to gain the most, the one with the means and the motive. Remember where I was at the time, imprisoned in my own domain... your poor old dad."

"Yeah, you've been misunderstood and mistreated. Cry me a river. You are completely made of bullshit. I don't believe a word."

"Trust must be earned, I get that," he said, sounding hyper sincere. "So, let me earn your trust. Let me bring the offender to justice. Let me prove myself."

I could not go on listening to his brainwashing voice. The danger was too grave. "Get the fuck out of my head, you geezer! How do I shut this off? How does my brother do it? I hope he kills you, by the way. No one deserves it more than that guy, the son you scorned and ruined for eternity."

"To do that, first he'd have to stick his head out of the festering hole he's been hiding in. A coward, that's his true nature. I have higher hopes for you."

I kept going, hoping to keep him distracted. "Why did you send that damn Earth troll? I know it was you. Was it some kind of test? Did I pass, dad?"

"Not my handiwork, but I couldn't be prouder of the way you handled it. You are truly of my blood."

"If you know what I need, then help me escape Darius's blackmailing clutches and that stupid wedding he has planned with his godson."

"I can kill them both in a breath, you say the word and it's done."

Fuck, he's useless.

"Is killing the only way you solve problems?"

"It's quick and to the point."

"Thanks for the tip," I said. "I'll keep it in my serial killer tool kit."

He laughed. "Leave the killing to me. Such things will be a burden to your naïve young mind."

"I might need to defend myself," I said. "According to my panther fiancé, many people are a threat to me, even my own father."

His voice became a whisper. "As long as my hand is never forced, child, you need never fear me."

Even hidden in a whispered assurance, I felt a threat down in the bottom of his deep voice. His words echoed an infinity of nuance.

Extracting every last ounce of the magic in my core, I shoved him out of my head and drew my shields up all around me. I could feel the intensity of the effort aching in my bone marrow.

I welcomed the sound of my ringtone. It was Aiyana from the pack. She informed me with great enthusiasm that the wedding rehearsal had been scheduled. It would happen two days from now at a secure venue.

It triggered a gag reflex.

I waited in my car for my anxieties to calm. I started the engine. My core felt corrupted, my mind invaded. *This is not my war to fight*, I kept thinking. I didn't have to follow through. I didn't have to unsettle Horror.

Milan Visser was an illusion, real face or not. Only Horror existed. Staying in his orbit would unsettle me, not him. Where did I ever get the audacity to think I could outplay him in a game of wits?

Oh, yeah, because delusions of grandeur run in the family.

Chapter 10

THE SWORD LAY ON the velvety loveseat unsheathed. I'd polished it so feverishly I could see my distorted reflection on the surface of the blade. My hair was braided into a low bun. My pistachio crepe dress with the spaghetti straps revealed two toned shoulders and arms. Not the black widow outfit I had in mind, but this was just the wedding rehearsal.

I'd brought the sword with me to Coronado Beach to feel close to Winter, and also because it would displease Cyrus. Pissing him off was the only delight I had left in this whole sordid affair.

I glanced outside through the arched window of the reception venue. A few scattered clouds lingered in the blue skies. Right on the sand, rows of white chairs adorned with golden ribbons were covered with clear plastic. A blue tarpaulin tent had been placed over the beautiful wedding arch that was decorated with white and red flowers.

Nobody consulted me about any of this. Not that I gave a single fuck.

At least twenty shifters marched across the beach, scanning the area for threats or vulnerabilities. A few more stood next to a fence at the other end of the reception venue. A large section of beach had been closed off to keep outsiders out. What kind of money had Cyrus spent on this fake ceremony?

Darius approached in long, assured strides. His lean, austere figure drew a stark contrast against the bountiful red rose bouquets, golden ribbons and colorful macarons that were used to decorate the venue.

He spotted the sword and frowned. "It's a quite lovely day," he said. "You should get out there and take a stroll in the fresh air."

I turned back to the window. "I'm all set, thanks."

"This is a moment to celebrate," he said. "You might not want to see it now, but our alliance will prove essential to both of us. We will be stronger together. Your desire for a just world will be bolstered. Against our united front, Horror will no longer pose a threat."

"If I have to hear these bullshit assurances one more time..."

Darius stepped closer. "I gave you time to adjust to your life with the pack. After the wedding, your education commences. I'll begin to reveal the true nature of your gift and how to reach beyond limits. One day you might even unlock the untapped power of the mist."

Goody. An old condescending male mentor.

"Speaking of gifts, I wish to offer my godson and his bride-to-be a wedding present like no other to seal this formal union of our two legacies. You may ask for the rarest of things and it shall be yours."

I considered his offer. "Okay, I want you to release Arsha," I said. "You promised to do it eventually. Well, now's the time. If that happens, I'll get you what you want, a wedding. And as a special bonus prize, I won't murder Cyrus in his sleep."

"Do that and your friends will suffer your choices."

"They're already suffering *your* choices."

He leaned in. "There are many levels of suffering. We haven't even scratched the surface yet. Believe me."

His threat game was no match for Horror's. I was over it.

"First an idle gift offer and now an idle threat," I said. "At least you're consistent."

His face contorted grotesquely. "I am not to be trifled with, Luna."

"Neither am I, Darius. Remember what I am."

We were at an impasse. He had no idea how tempted I was to reach through the mists of time to give Horror the green light to deal with Darius.

Aiyana interrupted us. A personal guard of Cyrus, she was dressed in a tight black leather dress and stiletto heels, her sleek dark hair reaching her waist. I was extremely jealous of her outfit.

"The ceremony rehearsal is about to begin," she said. "Lord Darius, the Higher Alpha has requested your presence in his dressing room."

Darius bowed and hurried out.

"I didn't like that energy," Aiyana said. "A bride should have only blissful thoughts before her wedding."

She had actually come to my rescue. I had no idea how much she knew, but it was obvious she didn't think highly of Darius.

"Lord Darius doesn't scare me," I said. "I do appreciate you sending him away, however. He's a complete drag."

She hesitated. "Your friend," she said. "I haven't seen him around the Keep. Is he okay?"

"*My friend?* You mean Carter?"

She nodded.

Carter, my faithful squire, was the only good thing to have come from my brush with Darius. When he was staying at the pack compound with me, Carter lavished Aiyana with attention and compliments and then disappeared when I advised him to run from Darius. I had no answers for her. Darius would slay Carter in a blink if he suspected his former student betrayed him to protect me. Carter's centuries of loyal service to Darius would mean nothing.

"I'm not sure what Carter's up to these days," I said. "He never settles down for long in the same place."

"I see," Aiyana said. "How about we get this show on the road?"

Carter had made quite an impression on her. I didn't see that coming. Only a fool would take his seductive overtures seriously. Aiyana was hard as nails and no fool.

I handed her my sword. "Can you hold this during the rehearsal?"

She raised an inquisitive eyebrow but took the sword.

Outside, staff had begun to remove the plastic covers from the first rows of chairs. The few shifter guests who weren't on the security team were ushered to their seats.

Darius stepped next to me. I wished I could say the look on his face was frustrated or sinister, but it was actually the most relaxed I had ever seen him. These manipulative shell games were how he had lived and ruled his entire Immortal life.

Darius put a big, strong hand on my arm. I fought a strong urge to kick him. It would be pointless, and I had promised Chaos I would not rock any boats no matter how tempting.

I glanced about the beach. The security guards had placed themselves in a circle around the small gathering, dressed in loose and casual clothes in order to be able to shapeshift at a moment's notice.

I caught a glimpse of Marlon. He was sitting near the back, cracking his knuckles, like a true henchman.

We stepped onto the long aisle runner that was laid out on the sand. Darius urged me forward to the wedding arch where Cyrus waited in an expensive tux with two body-guards on either side. I wasn't sure if this was going to be a wedding or a mob war.

Aiyana smiled to me from one of the front seats. My sword lay on the ground between her feet and under her chair.

Cyrus's eyes flashed red when I looked to him, then flared back to brown.

I fought to still the repulsion that rose in my gut. My fingers stiffened around the bouquet handed to me. All I wanted was to go back in time two months and start a bright new future with Winter.

I may have been walking towards a life inside a comfortable prison, but I was never the victim these people surely imagined me to be. I was a survivor trudging through the rubble of shabby options, trying to find jagged pieces of my fractured innocence and protect those I loved.

Cyrus flashed a grin, revealing two slightly crooked front teeth.

In the peripheral of my sight, something blue sizzled. I turned. My enchanted sword glowed through the sheath with an electric blue sheen. Aiyana's mouth hung open. The sword lit up like a firework as golden and purple sparks frenzied along the hilt.

My heart stopped. Winter broke through the perimeter of shifter guards, veins pulsing in his neck, blood stains all over his clothes and face. A guard reached for him but was shocked back by a cloaked energy field.

The sword slid out from Aiyana's chair, escaped its sheath and flew directly to Winter's hand.

My very own Shadow Warrior pointed the sword at Darius.

Darius's face went pale then red as shock was replaced by outrage. A woman screeched behind me like she was stabbed in the heart. Carter came into my field of vision, shoving a huge shifter guard forward with the tip of his sword.

"Winter," I managed to gasp, emotions flooding my senses.

"That's not fucking possible," Darius said, fixing his glare on Winter.

Winter weaved through flower arrangements to get to Cyrus.

The alpha shifter grabbed onto my hand, pulling me to him. I yanked my hand free and dropped the flower bouquet to stomp all over it.

"Have your security stand down," Winter said. "Let's avoid a bloodbath."

Cyrus was a tall, powerful man whose murderous gaze could freeze tough guys in their tracks. Right now, he looked like a child caught stealing.

He pursed his lips and said nothing.

"I'm not here to pick a fight," Winter said, "but if any of you get in my way, you'll be picking a fight which won't be much of one."

The guards closed ranks around Cyrus to protect him.

For a brief second, Winter and I gazed at each other. The world stopped spinning, and I sank into a pool of tranquility. The splash of the crashing waves and the lonely calls of the seagulls above were the only sounds besides the beating of my heart.

"How?" I said.

Winter winked at me. "Sorry it took so long."

The guards tore their clothes off. Their skin shone wet a second before their beast forms burst out of their human bodies in a flurry of shifting limbs and elongating bones. Their feral snarls made me suddenly shiver. I counted five wolves, two hyaenas, two badgers and one jaguar. They were twice the size of their animal counterparts.

Cyrus stood in the middle of the circle, unmoved, still in his human form.

The shifters growled, their mouths quivering

Winter kissed the blade of the enchanted sword. His face grew grim like he had pulled on a mask of death. The air felt thick with the promise of violence. Bloodlust flooded his eyes. He looked like a madman.

"I just cut down a dozen of Darius's elite Immortal warriors to put an end to this shitshow. So, go ahead, boorish howler, make my blade sing."

Cyrus's eyes blazed like two red stones on fire. "Stand down," he told his guards. "This is done. We're walking."

That's right, you prick. Go lick yourself and your wounded pride.

The shifters surged forward, breaking into a canter, protecting their alpha. Cyrus glanced back at me, then shifted in a flash, his black panther form massive, towering over the guards.

The staff had all vanished, hopefully before any of the shifting took place. Someone else had vanished, too. Darius the Undestroyable had run off like a frightened puppy with his tail between his legs.

Duly noted.

Aiyana was the only shapeshifter left on the beach, standing at the far end of the aisle runner. Her eyes brimmed with bewilderment and something else too, maybe curiosity. She exchanged glances with Carter.

"Go to her, you fool," I told my long-lost squire.

Carter strode to my side and fell onto one knee. "Daughter of the mist," he said, bringing my hand to his lips, "it's an honor to be back in your service."

"Okay, get up, you goofball," I said, pulling him to his feet. "I missed you, too," I said, hugging him. "I'll never be able to thank you enough."

Winter's rugged breath tickled my neck. I closed my eyes. I didn't dare to turn, afraid I was dreaming and turning would wake me up. Afraid he wouldn't be here.

But he *was* here. Not only that, but he had gone through the entire cycle of his restorative mode and was completely healed and revitalized. He had never looked stronger.

Winter's hand slid down my back.

Is this real? The Shadow Master said it would take years!

Winter stepped around in front of me, flowing like water. His blue eyes washed over me like a sheltering sky. He wore golden body armor stained with what looked like blood over a tight black outfit that hugged his body.

The last time I saw him, his thick blond hair was barely an inch long and spiked. Now long blond strands framed his face. His powerful body was corded with muscle as if he had been working out while in a coma.

"Good to see you, Luna Mae of Astoria," he said, his voice resonating with a deep subterranean current.

I'd forgotten how to form coherent sentences. A thousand fading words slipped under my tongue, unrealized. I stared up to him, dumbly.

I'm drowning in his eyes and his voice.

He studied me from head to toe. I knew what he saw. Soft fabric, pastel colors, a tense body and a dumb face with a smug expression.

"Your etheric essence is coiled," Winter said. "It might strike out at any moment and cut through your skin and rip that dress apart."

I smiled. "Hello, Winter. You look like a bloody savage king. A little gross but still... good."

And by good, I mean hot-as-fuck.

A sly grin on his lips came and went. "As usual, your timing is terrible."

A shadow moved across the roof of the reception venue.

"Someone's on the roof," I said, alarmed.

Winter turned slowly. "Yeah, I'm aware."

I looked closer. A familiar slick black trench coat reflected sunlight.

Chaos started running and jumped off the roof, the tails of his coat flapping behind him until he landed in a soft crouch.

He walked with a lazy swagger, his broad shoulders pulled back.

"You kept your promise," I said. "Whatever you did, I'm grateful."

He licked his lips. "I'd like to take the credit, little sister, but by the time I located the portal to the camp in question, Sir Melts a Lot was already gone. I tracked and caught up with him and the squire on their way to good old San Diego and briefed them on your unfortunate circumstances."

I glanced at Winter. "Help me understand. You're not only free but you completed restoration mode already? There was no way out and I was told restoration would take years."

"That's a long conversation we'll save for later. Right now, we need to get to the Umbra portal. The Shadow Master will seal it once we get there. Darius possesses too many secrets of the Order. Allowing him access to the Shadow Realm could be an apocalyptic mistake."

"And yet you let him live and breathe."

"Killing a demigod is not a light task. It requires considerable planning and resources. Fighting him in the basic world would be a seismic event. And, besides, I know your heart. In the end, you wouldn't let me kill him."

"I'm no longer that girl," I said. "I've grown practical. I see the big picture. I'm a bad bitch now. You should have killed them both."

"You don't mean that."

Didn't I?

"Wait, Jonas, what about Arsha?"

He tossed the sword aside and wrapped me in his arms. "She's on her way to Umbra, two trusted Shadow Warriors as escort."

I collapsed onto his chest. I felt like I had been holding a single breath for months. I exhaled all over his wide, armored chest, letting go of all the tension trapped in my body until the only things left to hold me up were my Shadow's lovely, powerful arms.

Chapter 11

THE HEAVY DOORS TO the Great Hall stood ajar at the end of the hallway. I took a deep breath to calm my frenzied heart. The last time I stayed at the Umbra fortress, Chaos had forced me to stand in front of the Council and lie to the Shadow Master himself. A few soul crushing months later, I was about to face the same Shadow Council. My presence, no doubt, was a bad omen. Every time I appeared, I brought disaster to the feet of the High Master.

I had run out of excuses to stall any longer. I had showered, put on the Umbra gown, and had a hearty meal before they called me to the assembly. I glanced at Nicolau standing next to me, the Umbra apprentice who had come to fetch me. His face was a blank sheet. I never saw even a glimmer of emotion register there.

"Strength is a state of the mind," I said and continued through the door.

The Great Hall was filled to capacity. Every Shadow Warrior in the fortress, every available member of the Council, and even three of the legendary Nine Elders had assembled. Dozens sat around the great rectangular table, but quite a few were left standing in rows all the way back to the walls.

The Shadow Master sat at the head of the table. Mohan, the grim Shadow Warrior who was the Master's right hand, sat by his side.

The three Elders occupied the other end of the table, sitting on some elevated platform, so they loomed over the congregation. They held onto silver staffs with the Umbra seal on top: a red U run through with a silver dagger. Although Immortals, they had aged themselves enough to brandish gray hair and skin dotted with deep spots and wrinkles.

The Superior Elder rested his cold eyes on me. His gaze was impossible to hold. A vast ocean of unfathomable wisdom and energy swam in those eyes. He could crush your shields in a breath. I looked away.

The Shadow Master rose. His fit, elegant presence filled the room with a regal radiance. His eyes were both gentle and inquisitive.

Winter, Chaos and Carter were at the table, too, sitting three in a row. The fact they allowed Chaos to sit at this table was a miracle. I looked for Arsha. She stood in her green gown in front of the vast bookshelves. She was pale, the golden halo of hair that had framed her sweet face gone. Her head was shaven clean. She bent her lips into a barely-there smile when our eyes met. We were the only women in the entire hall.

The Shadow Master fixed me with a formal stare. "The Umbra Council welcomes Luna Mae, esteemed member of the Lunar Order. Please, take your seat, young lady."

I scanned the table. I had a reserved seat between Winter and another Shadow Warrior. I was so strung out I hadn't noticed it at first.

Feeling all eyes on me, I made my way to the padded chair. Nostrils flared as the assembled took in my etheric scent. Winter pulled my chair back like a gentleman. By the time I sat down, my legs felt rubbery, like I'd walked a mile uphill.

Mohan rose. "We have requested the presence of our Lunar guest to bear witness to the misdeeds of Lord Darius. We understand, Luna Mae, that his duplicity and deceit have caused you great distress."

Am I supposed to respond? That felt more like a statement.

The Superior Elder thumped his silver staff on the elevated platform. "Speak your truth, child. Tell us of the Lord's treacherous scheming."

I knew if I told them anything, questions would arise, questions I could not answer. The fact that Darius had targeted me solely because I was much more than a lunar witch was the whole damned story.

Without talking to Winter in advance, we had zero chance to get on the same page and keep our stories straight. That was why they separated us the moment we were spewed out of the Umbra portal.

The Shadow Master knew I was a mist rider, but had he shared that knowledge? Did the Elders suspect? I decided to proceed with caution.

I cleared my throat. "Honorable Masters of the Umbra Council, I am truly grateful for the offer of shelter," I began. "I will tell you what I know. I am certain you will piece it all together better than I have. Lord Darius admitted to me he was the one who allowed Düsternis access to the Shadow Realm so that he could capture the Shadow Emrod, who sits among us now using the name Chaos. He also confessed to the kidnapping of Magistrate Winter and the Shadow Initiate Arsha. And then, drunk on power, he offered me up as a gift to his godson, Cyrus, the Higher Alpha of the San Diego shapeshifter pack, who intended to use me as leverage to augment his own power."

Not bad. Not good. At least I gave away as little as possible.

The Superior Elder again thumped his staff. His eyes glowed white. Shadow magic enveloped me in a poisonous cloud. I caught myself in time to pull back my own welling mist energy before it devoured the Elder's magic.

Color began returning to the Elder's eyes. "What proof is there to back your words, daughter of Selene? Lies have passed your lips before in this very chamber before this very council."

That's what I get listening to Chaos. A bad rep.

Winter tensed beside me. It was too late for his help.

"The Elders possess great powers of intuition. There is no use hiding the truth from you. Let Magistrate Winter speak. His truth will validate mine. He is the Master Warrior of the Shadow Arts. He does not lie. Everyone here knows that as well as I. And it was he who was most harmed by the treacherous behavior of Darius. There is no end to what Lord Darius would do in order to amass insuperable power. He'll stop at nothing to control all five realms and pull every last living thing into a final dark age where he reigns."

I looked about the table. Nobody stirred. You could hear me lick my lips.

So... tell them more, I guess.

"Murderous monsters," I blurted out, "and banished supernatural creatures are battling their way back into our worlds. The gates will not hold them back forever. The Deep Down has guarded the gates for centuries. We are in great peril. My people. All of our peoples. Is Lord Darius involved in that as well? Probably not a coincidence. We all have to stand together, Shadow Warriors, to figure this out, to protect the world."

Another Elder pounded his staff, more forcefully than the first. The magic hit me in the gut like a fist of bricks. I almost keeled over.

The Elder spoke. "What are we listening to? Who is this lowly witchling of the basic world who comes into our domain to instruct us on matters of hierarchy and the stability of the five realms? Her mind is clearly mush. What does she know about protecting worlds?" He glared at me. "You shall answer only what is asked or I will burn off your tongue."

I couldn't argue with him, or at least shouldn't. As an outsider, I should sit back and listen.

Except... screw it.

I rose to my feet. A collective grumble of disapproval rolled through the Great Hall. "A week ago, I fought an ancient Earth troll in the basic city of San Diego. I had to use tremendous energy to slam him back into the time portal from which he had escaped, and I had to do it without hesitation, or he would have trampled all over my city. I also had to conjure a spell to erase the event from memories across the globe. So, yes, I've been out there. That's who I am. I've dealt with one mess after the other, working my ass off trying to protect the world while you're having gatherings and scolding people on etiquette."

Winter's face turned red, his eyes widening from shock. I wasn't sure if it was because of my story about the Earth troll or my disrespectful reproach of all the ancients in the room. Both, I suspected.

"The gist of it, fellas," I went on, "Darius lied to you all and now he has vanished while the gates between the realms are being tested and breached. Are you going to do something about it? Because I'm exhausted."

A roar of indignation erupted in the Great Hall. The tension was palpable. I imagined the Shadow Warriors would combine their dark energies to vaporize me, and I was okay with it. I sat down until they decided.

I took Winter's hand under the table. He squeezed it for a second. That brief act of tenderness was all the encouragement I needed. Winter couldn't speak on my behalf, but no matter what I chose to do, he'd have my back.

I locked onto the Shadow Master's eyes. His lips pursed but his hard face was otherwise unreadable.

Arsha covered her head with her gown's hood and stepped forward. She bowed. "Shadow Warriors, I urge you to consider the words of Luna Mae. She understands the basic world better than any of us. Eyes raised outside the Shadow Realm can often see that world more clearly."

The Superior Elder thudded his staff so hard I thought it'd punch a hole through the platform. "This Luna Mae as you say, Initiate, claims to have contained a banished Earth troll. How did a lunar witch manage to do that and why did she delay in the telling of that information?"

"She should have never been allowed here," someone said.

"We're being fed lies," another said.

They should be used to that by now.

The Shadow Master banged both fists on the table. "I will have order in my Hall," he said. The voices quieted. "Luna Mae is a rare hybrid witch with electrokinetic training, and she can tap into ley line energy."

The Elder's eyes went completely black like oil. His lips quivered. He was having a vision. Only Umbra Elders could have visions and still keep talking normally. "That gives me nothing, High Master, but more questions. The witch spoke of controlling a time portal and erasing *basic* memories. That kind of stacked power never manifests in an entity outside the high ranks of Eternals. She was born in this young century."

The Shadow Master glanced around the Hall. "Perhaps we have more to learn, Superior Elder. Perhaps this is a question for the Great Chanter Horpheus who oversees all Orders in the Deep Down."

"Why did the troll appear to her?" a voice asked.

I tapped my nails on the table. "I can't be sure it's Darius, but whoever's forcing banished creatures into our world, they're doing it because of me. I'm certain of that. I'm the ultimate target they're trying to provoke."

I thought the Elder would have a stroke, if only he were mortal.

"You?" he said, confused now, sensing something more. "Why would you be the ultimate target of such unprecedented anomaly?"

Chaos sneered. "Ye Gods. So thick, the lot of you. Your master has turned himself into a pretzel trying to avoid telling you that this sickly girl, whose personality is a work in progress, is quite a bit more than a witch. You lucky idiots with your vacant expressions are still clueless that standing before you, right here and now, is in fact a Mist Rider."

Thanks, bro. Better you than me.

Winter exhaled, surprisingly relieved.

Chaos's words had stunned the room. The Superior Elder's pupils shrunk back to normal size. The three Elders leaned to each other, forming a huddle, to whisper among themselves.

My essence cloaking was straight fire. Up to this moment, the Elders were completely clueless about my true identity.

Winter rose. "The fallen Shadow tells the truth. I have guarded this secret for twenty-three years. A new rider of the dawn, bearer of the morning light, has been born into the world out of the mists of time."

"It was you, Magistrate, who cloaked her essence?" the Superior Elder said.

Winter nodded. "It was a necessity for the rider's safety. Dark powers are rising in-between the realms, my Lords, and the Dark Eternal is regaining his might. He cannot have access to the Rider until she finds her horse."

Well, a bit too late for that.

The Elders thudded their staffs all at once.

"It has been foretold," the Superior Elder said, "that the Dark Eternal shall rise to power again and claim the Divine throne above all beings."

"This is why the rider was placed in the shelter of the Lunar Order," the Shadow Master explained. "Why we have served to protect her."

Everyone started talking as if suddenly awoken from a mass coma.

The three Elders rose as one. Their robes flowed about them and then slid from their bodies to reveal golden armor underneath. Their hair darkened and their skin tightened and cleared up all blemishes. The Elders had shed at least forty years in appearance.

"The Elders will rise once again to fight by the side of the Mist Rider," they decreed in one echoing voice.

"As will the Shadow Warriors," the Shadow Master proclaimed. "Rise brothers of the half-light. Let there be a blood vote."

All Shadow Warriors rose, drawing their swords. They placed the blades against their palms and slashed their skin open. They dipped the tip of their blades in the blood and then yelled out a battle cry, "Alu! Alu!" They shook their bloodied swords over their heads.

The Master's deep voice reverberated off the walls. "Mist and Shadow will work as one against the emerging darkness. We swear allegiance, Daughter of the Mist. We are now your banner brothers by oath."

A round of applause followed his words. I felt hard pressed to say something witty but found the wisdom to shut up. My cheeks burned. The Elders and the army of Shadows needed me to be something I wasn't.

Not yet anyway. Maybe not ever.

Chaos leaned in to speak softly into my ear. "Order them to renew my club membership."

I shouldered him away. My mind was on overload. The

Shadow Warriors bowed their heads and then roared and beat their chests. It was a lot.

I grabbed Winter's hand. "Get me out of here," I said under my breath. "It's nice to have allies, but this is way too much testosterone right now."

Winter approached the Shadow Master to explain we'd be leaving. I stepped back from the table. Arsha led me out into the hallway.

"Everything has changed," she said. "Everywhere. In all the realms."

I hooked my arm with hers. "Arsha, I'm so happy you're safe." I glanced at her shaved head. "Did Darius do this?"

She rubbed her skull. "This? No, the Shadow Master did. In our realm, it's the highest of honors."

Guess that explained why the Shadow Master himself was bald.

"What does it signify?" I said.

"It means I've advanced to the next stage of initiation—the final stage." She smiled. "I will become a Shadow Warrior, Luna. The first woman in the Order's grand history."

Her words both exhilarated and troubled me.

"Luna? What's wrong?"

"Have they told you the final test?"

She laughed. "It's not the Middle Ages. Shadow Warriors can prove themselves in other ways besides killing someone they love."

"Thank goodness," I said. "And what a relief because I know just how lovable I can be. I feel safer now."

"You'll always be safe, silly girl. You stand with so many now."

Chapter 12

"How did you escape?" I said as Winter unlocked the condo door. "That place was supposed to be impenetrable. Darius had Immortal guards posted everywhere." I had been waiting for answers since Winter burst through the shifter guard perimeter at the wedding rehearsal, covered in blood.

We never talked on our way home. Even if he acted like nothing had changed, I knew Winter's mind was still in a dark place after the Nightwood battle and the remote prison camp of the Ten Thousand Immortals.

"I've lived long enough to learn every army's and every commander's weakness," he said, stepping aside to let me enter the condo first.

It was dark, like the first time I broke into his home. I had used his name's magic then to deactivate his wards. That had pissed him off big time.

Winter turned on a soft orange light. This time he didn't

wait in the hallway, wondering how I had entered. Instead, he spun around and took my hand, tugging me to him. He rested his chin on top of my head as I buried my face in his chest.

"These have been the longest two months of my life," he said, exhaling deeply. For a 3000-year-old man that said something.

"Oh, my poor sweet man," I said, putting my arms around him to squeeze with all my strength, needing to absorb his powerful physicality to reassure me that he was really here. "I'm so sorry Darius did that to you."

He winced, so I loosened my tight grip on him. Somehow, he was in pain.

"He did it to both of us," he said.

I studied his face. "You're still hurt. How is that possible?"

"I'll live," he said as he led me to the couch.

A year ago, it was I who had bled on that couch. Winter stabbed me to prove I couldn't die. My whole world changed that day.

"Sit," he said. "I need the bathroom."

He's hiding something. I'm not having that.

I found him, head in the sink, faucet pouring over his hair.

He didn't hear me as I entered. His shirt was off, so I had a clear view of his back. The tattoo of a bronze star at the base of his neck was gone, replaced by a long, fresh scab that hadn't healed. Drops of blood had oozed from the scab, leaking onto his shoulder blades.

"Winter," I said, touching his wound. "I'm worried now. Tell me why you're not healing."

He pulled away, reaching for a hand towel. "Don't sneak up on me like that, Luna. I could have hurt you."

My eyes landed on his chest. Winter's golden tattoo of a regal double-headed eagle that used to shine on his massive pecs was now replaced by damaged, red skin, poorly healed from severe burns or cuts.

I'd seen his flesh quickly regenerate many times before. Winter's body created new cells and collagen to heal lacerations instantly. The restoration cycle might not have finished.

"Let me look at that," I said. "This is nasty. You should see a doctor. I know a woman. If nothing else, she can prescribe pain killers."

"Not necessary," he said, turning to the mirror to examine the damage. "Not my first rodeo."

"It kind of is though," I said. "You've never needed a doctor before."

He placed my hands down on his hips. "How about we just play doctor. That sounds more fun. You make the loveliest doctor."

"Not happening," I said. "Games would wear you out and you need rest."

"Can I get a second opinion?"

"You're not fooling me, big guy. You're clearly trying to change the subject, which makes me more curious how you managed to escape all on your own. What did you do? What did it cost you? Did you make promises?"

"A friendly Earth troll materialized out of nowhere and pounded the shit out of my capturers," he said, taking me in his arms.

"You might have been unconscious for months, but I see you're still full of all the same old brutish bullshit."

"I need it to survive you," he said with a wink.

He's even hotter when injured and a total prick. I mean, really. Totally. Fucking. Edible.

"My healing rate," he said. "I've slowed it down on purpose. I need to keep the wounds raw for a while, so the tattoos won't regenerate."

"You removed them yourself?"

"I hacked them off."

Jesus. "You idiot. Why? That's gruesome."

"My desire to be a Magistrate has ceased," he said. "Upon resignation, you can no longer bear the council symbols on your body. I need to clean the wounds before I shower. Don't worry, Luna, it'll leave a scar but will heal properly in time. I have it under control."

"You know people who've lost control always say that."

"Well, I only say that when it's true. I've seen my share of battleground stitch-ups. It's all good in the hood. Your mind needs rest."

"You don't even know what I'm talking about," I said.

"That happens a lot."

I really wanted to slap his face. "Guess what, smartass? I was going to play doctor, but you blew that."

"So touchy," he said. "Hard to believe you're the same woman who held me in her arms on the battlefield."

"What? You remember me holding you?"

"Maybe," he said. "Only if you were the woman who said she loved me."

Oh, shit. He could hear while comatose.

"Must have been someone else," I said.

"That's true," he said. "Lots of candidates."

I punched his shoulder. "You jerk. How could you hear that?"

"Not my first coma," he said.

"Well, I guess I'm busted. I have terrible taste."

"Clearly," he said. "I..."

I didn't let him finish. I rose onto my tiptoes and kissed his lips.

"You were hurt," I said. "I wanted to say nice things."

He pulled me close. Our tongues met eagerly, swirling in tiny cyclones until I was breathless.

Winter put his forehead against mine. He liked to do that. I liked it more.

"Luna," he said with eager eyes, "they're just words. I've lived too long for words to have too much of an effect on me. I could say the very same words to you if I wanted to say nice things."

What's stopping you, foolish man?

He cupped my cheek with one hand. His lips traced the other side of my neck down to the collarbone.

"Cerber made me watch when the Eternal Warriors closed in on you," I said between breaths. "I saw them hack away at your body, your face, and I was helpless. The agony of watching you die destroyed me. For a cruel eternity I thought you were dead. I searched for your pulse. It was gone."

"I'm here now, very much alive."

I pulled back to look at him. "The Shadow Master said there was a chance you wouldn't recover and if you did, the damage would take years to heal. Yet, here you are, two months later, completely recovered."

He lowered his eyes. "Someday I'll explain it to you, I promise."

Someday? I'll give him a day or two, then I'll make him speak.

"Luna, are you in there?" Carter banged on the front door.

Winter furrowed his brow. "I think it's your watchdog."

"My squire," I corrected him. "Show some respect."

"Luna, open the door, I know you're in there," Carter barked.

Winter chuckled. "We both know he won't go away."

I sighed. "I'll talk to him."

Winter kissed me. "Tell the lad to respect my neighbors and keep his testosterone in check."

"Not going to work. He's all testosterone."

"The boy has no tact, no finesse, he's an unrefined beast."

"Precisely," I said, sticking out my tongue.

I opened the door a crack.

"Hey, why'd you ditch me at the portal?" Carter said.

I opened the door wide to let him in. "It's a bad time, Carter. Go catch up on sleep and we'll grab a coffee in the morning."

He seemed offended. "You know I can't leave you. After your big reveal, every supernatural entity with a power fantasy will be out looking for you. You'll need all the support you can get. It's my job to protect you."

"I'm perfectly protected in Winter's home. Like I said, we'll speak in the morning and figure out what we do next."

He looked at me with hurt eyes. "Fine, I'll stay outside the door. If you have a cushion and a small throw blanket, I'll spend the night out there."

"Dude, c'mon, not again!"

He crossed his arms. "You leave me with no choice."

Ugh.

I grabbed his sleeve and dragged him to the door. "I gave you a choice. Go down the street, there's a lovely hotel. Get a room, that's an order."

"A hotel?" he protested. "The Shadow Master didn't give me a pouch of golden coins when he sent me after you."

"I don't think they would take the gold coins."

"Exactly," he said.

"Aiyana's in town. I see the way you two look at each

other. I'll text you with her info."

He frowned. "I would never impose on her again."

Great. Now he chooses to act chivalrous.

I handed him my keys. "Here. Spend the night at my place."

Winter appeared at the end of the hallway, leaning against the wall, his arms crossed over his chest. He had pulled on a wine-red colored shirt and had brushed his wet hair back. He looked insanely handsome.

Carter bowed. "Magistrate, my charge is being stubborn."

"Ha. Does that surprise you, squire?" he said.

As charming as ever.

"It does not, sir."

"I shouldn't think so," Winter said.

"You're both not funny," I said.

"Who was trying to be funny?" Carter said.

"Listen, I can assure you, noble squire, your charge will be perfectly safe here under my protection," Winter said. "And I have a different errand for you. I would like you to deal with Cyrus McDonnell. Make sure the message is strong enough to reach Darius."

Say what? "Hold on a second. What do you mean *deal with Cyrus?*"

"Carter knows what I mean. And if you asked Cyrus, he'd know it too. In fact, he wouldn't expect anything less. He knows I'm coming for him, and he would do the same."

I shook my head. "No, uh-uh, there will be no more

violence on my account. *Nada*."

Winter's face turned stone cold. "Did that bastard lay a finger on you? How far did he intend to take that wedding charade?"

I exhaled so hard I thought fumes would shoot from my nostrils. "I'm not going to have some jealous macho psychopath defending my honor. I defend my own honor. I'm perfectly capable of dealing with Cyrus when and if I ever find the time." I punched Carter in the arm. "What I'd really like to know is how you two thorns in my side ended up together?"

The two men exchanged glances. They clearly had forgotten to get their stories straight.

"Darius has enemies even among his own men. I negotiated until I got a lead on Arsha's location," Carter said. "I did not expect to also find the Magistrate there."

"When was that?" I said, turning to Winter. "Were you healed by then?"

Winter's face lost all mirth. He looked at me with a telltale dark glow in his eyes. "I'd been slowly regaining strength and focus for days yet remained still, waiting for the right moment. When Carter showed up at the camp, I assumed you had sent him."

"I wish I could take credit," I said with regret, "but that was all Carter."

"When Carter entered my tent, I knew it was time to act. The camp teemed with tremendous amounts of raw power at levels higher than even Serenity Valley. Never felt anything so powerful outside the Umbra and the Eternal Halls. Darius's Immortals do not have the capacity to fully engage all that energy, but I do."

"Your Shadow training?"

He hesitated. "In part, yes, but it's a bit more complicated. I had gathered just enough strength by then. Carter took out the men guarding my tent, while I unleashed a series of staggering waves of unbridled energy onto the camp."

Carter's eyes went all starry. "The Earth shuddered and widening cracks sliced the ground like a mega earthquake. The cracks became huge gaps at least twenty feet wide running across the entire camp, swallowing up parts of the buildings, tents and guards alike. Fire shot out of the gaps, detonating a series of explosions. During the mayhem that ensued, we cut our way through those left standing."

Hundreds if not thousands of Immortals must have been trapped inside the Earth.

Winter raised his eyebrows. "I had to anchor some of the energy onto a buffer so it wouldn't backfire and fry me on the spot. Carter provided that buffer. Darius will be busy for some time salvaging what's left of his army."

I glanced at Carter. "It could have killed you. Both of you. Carter, you're reckless and brave like most heroes. I know Darius convinced you that serving as squire was the best place for you, but it's not true. I release you immediately of those duties. We will fight side by side one day, my dear friend, of that I am certain. And we will do so as equals."

Carter bowed slightly. "Impossible. You have no equal, but I get it. I will leave you both in peace."

He pivoted, spun and walked out.

I bit my finger, piecing together what I had heard. "One thing bugs me," I told Winter. "Darius is no fool. Why did he ever take you to a place where so much power would be at your disposal? He certainly knew you'd eventually find a way to use it against him."

He shrugged. "That's right, but he thought he had years."

I frowned. "Everyone did, Jonas."

He sighed. "I know you have more questions. Not everything has an explanation, Luna. You just have to roll with it. My body tapped into old, taboo magic while I was comatose. I'd rather not have used it, but I was out of options. There may be repercussions, I just don't know what."

We were at that place again. Winter really didn't want to go into details about how he had recovered so fast, or how he had managed to tap into all that energy right away. I wasn't sure I really wanted to find out.

We sat on the couch. Winter put his arm around me.

"It will either be okay," he said, "or we'll make it okay."

"At least I'm done hiding what I am."

He arched an eyebrow. "I wish that gave me the sense of relief I see it has given you. Let's not forget, Horror's still out there."

"Yeah, about that... Horror, too, is aware I'm a mist rider.

When you lost consciousness in battle, Horror joined the fight. He saw me. We talked. He asked me to join him. He might have kidnapped me if Darius, the Shadow Master and Chaos hadn't intervened to stop him."

Winter closed his eyes. "It's too soon," he said. "We're not ready."

"I don't think he wants to kill me," I offered. "Not yet. We can stall him."

"We'd only be stalling the inevitable."

He wasn't the only one reluctant to tell the whole story. I needed to come clean and tell him that the deaths of Helen and his son were not accidents, and that Horror was my father and had tricked his way into my San Diego life. I knew I had to tell him, but not today. Eventually, sure, but I couldn't bring myself to do it on the day he had returned to my arms.

When he spoke again, his voice was growing weary. "I want you to move in here, with me. We're better as a team. And the next time a monster comes for us, we'll vanquish the odious scourge together."

Chapter 13

MUFFLED VOICES WOKE ME up. My heart pounded in my chest. I'd dreamed I was burning alive, then my wounds healed, and the burning started all over again.

I found Kirsi with Winter in the living room. She threw me an apologetic glance. "I'm sorry I woke you, but I'm too excited right now," she said.

I smiled. "That's good, right? Don't be sorry."

She grabbed Winter's shoulder. "This guy. I knew he was made of tough fiber and a shitload of Shadow grit, but this resurrection is next level epic badassery even for our Ice God."

"Shit happens," Winter said, peeling himself off the couch.

Kirsi looked at me. "Right as rain. Fucking unbelievable."

Winter made his way to the door. "Ladies, I'd love to stay and chat..."

I cut him off. "Bullshit happens. You don't want to stay."

"Not at all," he said with a grin, "but I do have some things to catch up on."

"You're no fun," Kirsi said. "I was going to order IHOP for breakfast."

"Raincheck," he said and shut the door behind him.

Kirsi turned to me with her face scrunched. "He does not behave like a man who had sex. I bet you made him talk all night."

I forgot about her ability to read body language.

"Not all night," I said. "We got a few cuddles in there."

Her jaw dropped. "Cuddles? I bet that's what he was hoping for after months away from you. You do realize that is a man of the male gender?"

"How about some coffee?" I said to drop the subject.

Kirsi followed me to the kitchen. "I expected thunder to roll down Mount Olympus last night and Thor's hammer to blaze through the skies, but it was a quiet night."

"Do you want to die, Valkyrie? It's a bit risky for us to, ah, comingle. You know that, so stop being a nasty ho."

"I was hoping you'd found a solution to that pesky little problem of yours by now," she said. "Can't you see the Erotes? They might have a fig leaf to rub on it, or some saffron gel, or maybe a magic hazelnut to swallow that will shield such dark unions from connecting to the energy spheres."

I had to nip this in the bud. "It's not a problem." *It is so a problem*. "Sleeping next to him after thinking I'd lost him forever will have to do."

She pursed her lips. "You know, there are things you could try that might produce only minor energy reverberations."

I rolled my eyes. "Thank you, Miss Freud. I'll thank you to use that imagination in your own sex life."

"Okay, okay, I just worry about you lovebirds."

I breathed in the smell of the coffee grounds. "Did Winter mention anything about going after Cyrus?"

"He seemed more concerned with Darius," Kirsi said. "He thinks we're missing an important piece of the puzzle."

"Just one, huh?"

"Listen, Luna, I actually came with information."

I put my coffee mug down on the counter. "You found something."

"Not something, someone. Guess who showed up when I was down at the Seventh Council Courts digging through the Ephemera Almanacs."

"Santa Claus? Bigfoot? Ringo Starr?"

"Brace yourself," she said. "It was that hag Chazona."

I was so stunned Kirsi reached out to touch my arm.

"Why was she there?" I said.

"She was there to yell at me like a lunatic. She threatened to report me to the Librarian Magistrate. Phony bitch was out of her fucking mind, spraying spit and everything."

The wheels in my brain started spinning. Chazona had the motive, she had pursued Winter throughout the ages. She definitely had the opportunity and the means.

"Honey, try to blink," Kirsi said.

"You don't think—?"

"It's hard not to. Just before she showed up, I'd found a reference to the accident. I had my hand on the file when Chazona stormed in like a bat out of hell. After I straightened things out with the Librarian, I went back. The file was gone, Luna."

That jealous giraffe!

"She took it, obviously."

"Either she or one of her flunkies."

My blood raged inside my veins. "If she's responsible for this, I'm going to tear her limb from limb."

"Either she did it or she's covering for someone." Kirsi unsheathed her sword and looked at her reflection in the blade. There was adoration in her eyes. She loved that sword. "There's only one way to know for sure. I'm going to confront her. I'll tell her I have conclusive evidence. She has a temper that can melt down titanium rods. She's likely to slip up."

I shook my head. "I worry she'll make a quick escape if you do that and have time to come up with an alibi, instead of us going straight to the one person who needs to hear the truth."

"We can't go to Winter with a suspicion," Kirsi said. "We need to put enough pressure on her, so she'll incriminate herself."

Madness this way lies.

"Chazona can't know we're working together or that we're on to her. We wait until we have enough evidence."

"Fine, we keep the slow-moving detective thing going," she said. "For the record, I think it's a mistake to wait. I prefer a good physical altercation."

"I know you do," I said, then tapped the edge of the counter with my fingernails. "Here's the thing, Kirsi. After Winter came back, we went straight to the Umbra Order. We told the council I'm a mist rider."

Kirsi's mouth curled into a frown. "Fuck, Luna, why'd you do that?"

"It's math," I said. "My enemies know. I might as well balance the scales with some allies."

"Umbra isn't exactly a paragon of virtue. Their idea of the greater good starts and ends with their own good. Throughout the ages they have planted more than a few knives into naïve backs."

A few months ago, I might have agreed, but the Shadow Master was a man of integrity. I trusted him to do the right thing.

There was a knock I recognized at the door. Carter. He rushed inside before I could even say hello.

"Winter's wards are down again," he said. "That's reckless, Luna." He spotted Kirsi on the couch. His face brightened. He bowed so low I thought strands of his hair might reach the floor. "Supreme Valkyrie," he said, "such a pleasure to be in the presence of your breathtaking beauty again."

Kirsi squeezed the grip of her sword. Something wicked sparked in her eyes. "I'm out of practice," she said. "Do you want to take this to the bedroom, so we don't disturb Miss *Virtue-is-my-middle-name* over there?"

Carter pulled his sword out. "Nah, she needs to see this."

The fuck?

"First blood," Kirsi said.

Carter nodded, revealing his teeth.

They picked up speed and met at the middle of the living room. Carter kicked the coffee table out of the way. Their swords touched.

Immortals doing Immortal stuff.

They slashed at each other, dodging, lunging, parrying back and forth. Kirsi was light on her feet, spinning and stepping aside to avoid Carter's heavy attacks like she was a ballerina.

I hurried out of the way and onto the desk by the window.

They clashed again and again, plunging into an avalanche of strikes and blocks, their movements syncing into a fluid rhythm, their swords natural extensions of their arms. Watching them spar, even in such a confined space, was spectacular.

Kirsi managed a low lunge, her blade coming within a millimeter of Carter's stomach. Her grin was that of a thrilled demon.

Carter stumbled back, amusement on his face. He

reversed the grip on his sword to bring it down and charged at Kirsi with a flurry of powerful strikes. Kirsi blocked every single one, spun on her feet and sliced Carter's left biceps.

"First blood," I announced the obvious. "Stop this at once."

Carter wiped the blood off his arm with the grip of his sword. The wound was healing already. A strange expression stretched over his features. Delight mixed with respect and something else—an invitation for more maybe? Whatever it was, he had enjoyed sparring with the Valkyrie a little too much.

"Thank you for not slashing into the shirt, fair Valkyrie," he said as he sheathed his sword. "It's the only one I own."

"You wield fine metal, and you know how to use it," Kirsi said. "Perhaps we can have a real match someday."

I shook my head. *No, Kirsi, don't go there.*

"Anytime," Carter said. "I look forward to it."

"Fair warning, in a real match, I won't stop until your clothing is in tatters and you're standing before me as naked as the day you were born."

An impish grin curled his lips. "Sounds like I can't lose."

I glanced at Carter. The idiot would let Kirsi win on purpose. "Okay, that conversation is over. Carter, tell me you didn't go anywhere near Cyrus."

"When did you become nanny to the shifter alpha?" Kirsi said. "That dirtbag deserves anything and everything he has coming."

"Yes, but when dispensing justice on one shifter becomes an act of war, that's on us. We don't need shifters everywhere going berserk. That would be a punishment to everyone, and it would make Cyrus into a fucking cult hero."

"Don't worry, I didn't go anywhere near the shit stain," Carter said.

"Yes. And, Carter, remember, you and I are a team. Don't just go off and do whatever Winter tells you because he's a cool Shadow legend."

"His ideas all lead to good, honest sword fun," Carter said.

"Still. Promise to run it by me first."

He rolled his eyes. "Is that us being equals?"

"Yes," I said. "We both have to agree on warlike activity."

"She's like that," Kirsi said with pride in her eyes. "A give-peace-a-chance girl."

I put my head face down on the desk, trying to level off the dizzying rollercoaster of the past 48 hours. It was times like this when my limitations overwhelmed me. Who was I to advise and lead living legends that were hundreds and thousands of years older than me? My only experience was working at a college coffee shop.

"Um, maybe we should give Luna some privacy," Kirsi said.

"Where should we go?" Carter said.

Kirsi looked at her phone. "I'm actually late for a date."

Carter's hopeful mood sank like a shot bird. "Yeah, I guess I should go on and buy myself some clothes."

"I thought you had no money," I said.

He shrugged as if that explained everything.

Kirsi squeezed my arm. "I'll be in touch."

As soon as Kirsi left I turned to Carter. "Did you really think you were going to hook up with a Valkyrie?"

"Luna, it's a game. I know she's not into me."

"That's good to hear, Carter, because sometimes I worry you've regressed into an extreme delusional state."

Carter peeked out the window. "Is Kirsi dating a mortal? Hey, is that the Magistrate down there?"

I joined him. Down below, standing on the sandy La Jolla beach, Winter and Chazona were deep in conversation, watching the waves of the Pacific as they lapped onto the beach a few feet away. Chazona's long, blonde hair fell down her back in lush cascades. Her tight outfit revealed every inch of her slender and sleek body.

The nerve of that thirsty bitch!

She was probably telling him she was worried about him and needed to see with her own eyes that Winter was alive and well, but I knew the real score. She was here to make sure Kirsi hadn't spilled the beans yet, or to do damage control if she had.

I ran down the stairs to meet them. Carter expertly slid down the rail.

Chazona saw me first. I looked for signs of annoyance or dismissal in her demeanor, but her face remained calm and controlled. It was almost as if she had rehearsed this moment.

Winter smiled.

Buddy, you're so busted.

"Luna," Chazona said. "I heard Winter's return ruined your wedding plans. I hope the groom isn't too heartbroken."

I gave her a maniacal grin. "He'll have to adjust quickly, especially since I'm moving in with Winter."

There she was. The calm façade cracked. Fire sparked inside her blue eyes, her mouth curving into a derisive smirk. She caught herself and eased back from her crazy.

"I'm a woman. I've been there," Chazona said. "Going from one man to another man so quickly though. Perhaps you should fly your independence flag for a while."

Carter pinched the back of my arm.

Yeah, yeah, I'm not going to let her goad me into frying her ass.

Winter looked miserable. He wanted this conversation to end.

"Your concern as a woman is appreciated," I said.

Carter stepped forward. "Have we met before?"

Chazona arched an eyebrow. "I don't think so."

"Yeah," Carter said, "I would have remembered."

Flirt with her and you're both dead.

Carter stepped back. Maybe he heard the growl inside my skull.

"Perhaps I shouldn't judge," Chazona said. "After all, you are new to the world. Every handsome man who showers attention on an inexperienced woman can throw her off balance."

The ice queen said all that looking at Winter, not me.

I reached behind me to clutch Carter's sword. He removed my fingers one-by-one from the sword grip.

Winter's face assumed a neutral expression. "I just got back," he said. "How about we call a temporary armistice before you bite into each other?"

Chazona feigned surprise. "She bites? Something picked up from that feisty animal she was engaged to, no doubt."

I smirked. "That was almost clever," I said. "Winter, I'll see you later."

Carter directed me back to the condo. "Let's go, don't look back."

"Stop pushing," I said. "I'm going. Sheesh."

I had to question Winter's judgement if he counted the ice queen among his friends. What would he do if he found out Chazona may have played a role in the death of his lost love and their son? There was a dark side to Winter—so dark it still frightened me. I saw it, I felt it, I barely survived it. There's no telling what depth of viciousness could be unlocked by such pain.

I hoped we were wrong about Chazona. Winter had been through enough. For humans, memory becomes a river of lost things. For Immortals, that river becomes a sea.

Chapter 14

THREE BIG PACKAGES WAITED for me stacked against my apartment door. There were no shipping labels that I could see from a safe distance. These had been dropped here without the help of a courier or the postal service.

I gathered energy in my palms and closed my eyes to scan the parcels for traces of a supernatural etheric charge. The boxes felt safe enough unless they were boobytrapped by basics. That would be above my paygrade.

When I unlocked the door, the apartment air felt normal—no unfamiliar essences or auras lingered about. Setting the packages on the coffee table, I quickly conjured a series of simple wards to shield the door and the windows.

I'd come to the apartment to gather some of the clothes and books I'd left behind before I had moved into the pack compound.

I sat on the couch and opened one of the packages. I

removed a few sheets of pink tissue paper to get to the contents. I stared in disbelief at three different pairs of pants: black boyfriend-cut and dark-wash skinny jeans, and a pair of beige slacks. They looked expensive and were perfectly sized.

I moved to the second package. White and black tees, two breezy tanks, a dressy blouse with a V-neck and bell sleeves, a thin ruby-colored cardigan and a lovely navy-blue shift dress.

What's even happening right now? This can't be real.

I found a pair of white Chuck Taylor sneakers, sandals and a black leather belt inside the third box.

Who could have left all that stuff for me? Winter was the obvious answer, but last night I agreed to move in with him. Why would he have anything delivered at my apartment? Kirsi maybe? I couldn't picture the leather loving Valkyrie shopping for casual and girly outfits. Lucia and Lily? No, they wouldn't risk leaving all that expensive stuff on my doorstep. They would deliver them right to my hands.

Which reminded me... I had to find a way to tell my best friend and her cake-baking mother I wasn't getting married after all. That should be a fun conversation. They were as excited about the wedding as I was mortified.

I dug through the boxes, crumpling up wrapping tissue and emptying all contents on the couch. I found an envelope at the bottom of one of the boxes.

I pulled out the card inside and read it:

Childhood is the real magic. I regret not having been there.

You would have wanted for nothing.

Shit! I dropped the card like it was red-hot and backed away.

The front door popped open. Milan Visser stood in the doorway dressed in an elegant gray suit clutching his briefcase, my wards flaring around him like wild red flames.

"Invite me in so I don't dismantle your toys, flower."

A lump formed in my throat. "Careful, you're losing your accent."

"No point in all that. You know who I am."

"Yes, you're sperm donor. And you're the psychopath who killed an innocent woman, my friend, Penelope, because she outsmarted you."

His eyes flashed with a deep angry purple. "One should not spend their whole life complaining about past events. We covered that topic. Let's proceed forward into the fresh air of the here and now."

"I suppose that's a convenient life strategy for anyone whose entire past was a reign of terror," I said. "What evil deeds for today? Did you come to kill your own daughter?"

"I came to talk," Horror said. "Nothing more."

"That's funny, because I have nothing more to say."

The coolest green I'd ever seen glistened in his eyes. "This would all go much more pleasantly if we keep it civilized."

I scoffed. The most diabolical Eternal who had to be exiled not to destroy all of civilization wanted to *keep it civilized*. I raised my hand. My wards flashed bright red for a moment before shuttering to the floor. Horror stepped inside with an impatient sigh. His magic filled the room like a soft rain-cloud that could burst into a downpour at any moment.

The door slammed shut behind him.

"That wasn't so hard," he said. He studied my tiny apartment. "Tell me, Luna Mae, is this how you've lived your whole life? Hunkered inside an ill designed room?"

"I love my apartment," I said. "And I don't hunker."

"Thus said the brainwashed masses of a faux capitalist state."

"Did you come to discuss failed political ideals?"

"I came to answer your questions. I told you I would."

"Alright, I have a question for you. Did you send your elite Eternal Warriors to Nightwood to kill Winter?"

He made a dismissive gesture. "Let's just say they got a little carried away. But I have heard the Magistrate is on his way to total recovery, so all's well that ends well, is it not?"

A lightbulb flashed in my head. "It was you. You're the reason he has healed so fast."

He ignored me completely and instead walked over to the now half-empty bookshelves. "A paltry collection of books, daughter. And I was led to believe you were quite studious."

He might have been done answering, but I wasn't done asking.

I might as well poke the wasp's nest. "Are you using me to get to Chaos? Did you expect him to warn me so you could finally have his location?"

"I wouldn't give one single shilling for information about a mongrel," he said. "I'm too busy enjoying my newly attained freedom."

"It's funny. For someone who's supposed to be all powerful, you really haven't a clue about your own son. You fail to see how the events of his childhood shaped his mistakes. Neglect. Terrible parental role models."

His magic rose like hot lava, burning against my own magic core. The feeling was unpleasant but, at the same time, it felt natural, like my blood was hungry for Horror's ancient, dark energy.

"I took that bastard son under my wing and tried to elevate him to Eternal status. He proved unworthy not only of my attentions but also of existence altogether."

Bastard. I knew he meant it literally. For all his refinement, Horror was still stuck in the dark ages.

"Really? And it's not because my mother preferred him to you?"

His eyebrows came together. "I risked my freedom by stepping into the basic world. That's what I'm willing to do to help you, but you need to ask questions that have answers."

"You mean, you will only answer the questions that will help you manipulate me."

He lifted his hand and energy sparked.

Fear took hold and I cast around me the best shield I could conjure.

Horror laughed. My fridge door suddenly opened and a bottle of spring water flew out, racing from the kitchen right into his hand.

"Your temper is tedious, my child. Perhaps you should consider using it more sparingly and keep it for when it might do a bit of good."

Couldn't he have just walked to the fridge? Had he really risked using his third eye vision and then magic to get a bottle of water?

Who does that?

"Do you know why you exist at all?" he said, twisting the top off the bottle. "Because I willed you into existence."

"You were bored," I said. "So, you made a kid?"

"Banishment grows old instantly. I was there for centuries. Out of a sense of mercy, I never wanted offspring," he said and then took a drink of water. "You see, Eternal progeny tend to lust attention or go mad or both before finishing puberty. That kind of staggering power granted at birth can corrupt an innocent mind and pervert their perception of reality. They often become outlaws or dangerous zealots or bloodthirsty miscreants. Emrod, or Chaos as he so distastefully calls himself, was a cosmic accident, but you... you could be my finest achievement. The day you were born, I poured my most luminous magic into your energy core. Does that sound like I wished to harm you?"

My heartbeat accelerated. I started breathing heavily in-and-out through my nose trying to calm myself.

"It sounds like I'm Frankenstein's monster." I said.

"Ah, you have read a few books. That creation was malformed and witless. You are strong of mind and pure of energy. I was to chisel you to perfection by my own hand: strong, fearless, loyal. And then that cowardly aberration stole you from your crib. He stole you away because he knew I had imbibed your cells with far more power than he could ever possess. Your brother is the villain who wanted your power. He instructs you to view your own father as an enemy."

Now I laughed. "It's astonishing you have cast yourself as the victim and your own abandoned children as the heartless abusers."

He spun the Thespian ring on his finger before sliding it off. He admired it briefly, then set it on the counter.

My father's magic, freed from the ring's constraints, sprung from him as a lush, blue mist.

My mouth dried up as oxygen thinned. He would hit me with everything he had. It was too late to run. I enhanced my shield, squeezing every drop of available energy into it.

Horror removed his blazer and rolled up the sleeves of his linen shirt. He leaned forward and bent his arms at the elbows. Tendrils of silver mist oozed from his skin and coated his hands and arms. He thrust his hands forward. His magic fizzed and flashed blue sparks. I backed away toward the door.

A silver mist flew up and hung suspended between us. It hissed louder as it formed a translucent triangle of energy containing a hologram.

Inside the hologram, the form of a woman emerged. She became more and more real. Her hair was styled into a bob-shaped bouffant, and she wore a blue button-down shirtwaist dress—both were fashions of the fifties.

Another woman materialized next to her. Chazona.

"I can't do it," the woman said. "I don't have it in me."

Chazona's face hardened. "Soon you will die and rot. Do as I ask and at least you'll leave a living legacy to the ones you love. You can say no, but the result will be the same. Only difference will be that your family will not have the money agreed upon. Decide quickly, I don't have patience for your indecision."

All the charm of a snake.

The woman swallowed. "And I won't have to kill anyone?"

Chazona gripped the woman's hand. "You drive the cab to Lake Murray at the specified time. Leave the rest to me."

The hologram fizzled out. I closed my eyes, trying to hide how much the glimpse into the past had shaken me.

"A question answered and a fear realized," Horror said.

"This could be another one of your tricks."

He pulled an ochre envelope out of his briefcase. "I believe this is the file your Valkyrie was trying to find. It's all there, not spelled out, but easy to extract if you know what you're looking for."

I took the envelope, almost mechanically. The doors of perception had swung wide open inside my head.

"You left the messages for Kirsi," I said. "You've coordinated every step of this fool's errand. I'm willing to bet you even tipped off Chazona that Kirsi was digging through the Ephemera Almanacs, so we'd connect her to this."

"Aye. You were taking longer than I hoped."

"Was the journal even real? And the professor was obviously clueless to having hired a sadistic god to be his lawyer."

Horror beamed. "He has never set eyes on me. The journal is quite real, but the professor has no idea it was ever removed from his safety deposit box. I replaced it with an exact duplicate."

His confession puzzled me. "You went to a lot of trouble with this whole charade, what did you hope to gain?"

He shrugged. "I wanted to do right by you."

"I can see you almost believe that, but you're really just trying to launch yourself into my life. You want something in exchange for the information."

"Why must I want something?"

"It's your nature."

"Dear girl," he said, "your shield is draining your energy core." He slipped the Thespian ring back onto his finger. His magic shrank, absorbing back into his cells. "You can drop the shield," he said. "Whoever told you I wish to harm you wanted us to weaken each other in battle." His face took on a sincere regret. "Daughter, I have no wish to control you. On the contrary, I want to infuse you with even more power."

"To arm me with more weapons, you mean."

"Not weapons, defenses. I did not dare hope I would procreate a mist rider, but my heart is swollen with pride. It is my job as a father to keep you safe and help you reach your potential. You are incorruptible. No amount of power can tempt a mist rider. I can open up the most devastating magical reserves in you, knowing full well you will not misuse it."

I didn't know how much longer I could remain civil. The Eternal who gave necromancers the ability to build undead armies of soul swallowers had concerns about misuse of power.

Spare me.

"Maybe my mother's genes led to my dawn legacy. Maybe you have nothing to do with it. Where is dear old Mom? I'd like to meet her."

He finished his water and tossed the empty bottle to the trash. The lid of the trash receptacle opened magically just in time to let the bottle land inside.

Unfortunately, it was not where I put the recyclables. I walked to the trash can, opened it and removed the bottle. I rolled my eyes at him and then tossed the bottle into the lidless can next to it.

"Your mother, dear soul, had her heart broken utterly and completely when you were snatched away by the bastard fiend. It is my hope that one day she will make contact."

Once again, he played dumb, pretending to be unaware of my mother's part in my abduction. I didn't know if he was conning me or himself.

"Such an optimistic fellow," I said, drenched in sarcasm.

Horror fixed his eyes on mine. Even subdued, his power tickled against my skin. "I need to make you stronger, fair mist rider."

"Would that be a good move for your ultimate survival? Or perhaps it would be your fatal mistake?"

"Didn't your folksy grandmother in Oregon teach you not to prejudge a person before getting to know them? You are driven by a political caricature perpetuated by the Eternals and their operatives in the Deep Down."

"Well, I have some first-hand experience with you now. You are the man who murdered an innocent old lady for having the wrong ancestors. You are also the man excited to murder his own son. Judgement rendered."

His one-sided grin chilled me. "The complex machinations of natural divinity are hard to assess by a young mind. Enemies and sycophants have plotted against me my entire tenure as the strongest Eternal. One sign of weakness is all they would need to pounce like a pack of supernatural vultures until they stripped me of my very essence."

"We all have problems," I said. "I can't help you. I'm not going to be groomed by some old psycho dude. Please leave and leave me alone. Do your dark deeds discreetly if you must, but out of my sight. I'm a grown ass woman and you were never a father of mine. So, please, do me a favor, fuck off."

"It does not surprise me that you are spirited," he said. "It pleases me. We have time. A perk of being Immortal, but until you come around you will always be at mortal risk. I don't want you at risk as I have a profound affection for you."

Ew.

I buried my forehead in my hands and rubbed my temples. "Okay, it's time for you to go. You allowed Cerber to come for me. The sheer amount of pain and misery he caused me. And that's your profound affection?"

Horror walked to the door. His expression suddenly changed. "Your squire... he's outside this door. I'd say he heard too much."

Carter, no!

Horror opened the door. Carter stared at us as his hand gripped his sword.

"Rest easy, toy soldier, I'm not in a mood for extermination," Horror said.

We watched him walk down the hallway to the stairs.

Carter's face was mortified. "How long have you—"

"Since Nightwood."

"He'll kill you, Luna. Maybe not today, maybe not this year or century, but eventually he will."

"He will try," I said, then became deeply concerned. "Carter, you need to forget about all of this. Immediately. Tell no one. Do you hear me?"

His eyebrows pressed together. "Winter doesn't know?"

"No, and you're not going to be the one who tells him.

He'd react in the most obvious way and end up dead. Again."

"I won't say a word, upon my honor," he said. He put his sword away, exhaling deeply. "Follow up question though. Is there then a plan knocking around in your head as to how the rest of us, you, me, any who dare stand in Horror's way, may not end up dead?"

"Um," I said in a daze, "I'll have to get back to you on that."

Carter nodded. "Please do."

Chapter 15

Carter pulled over at a 7-Eleven. "Just have to grab some Monsters," he said.

I stared at him. *Huh?*

"Monster Energy," he clarified. "You know, the drink."

Ah.

"You need to get even more hyper?"

He shrugged. "Feeling sluggish. Need a pick me up."

"Okay, go," I said.

He ran into the convenience store.

Should an Immortal really prescribe himself canned energy from 7-Eleven?

I watched a teenage girl with blonde and pink hair vaping across the parking lot. My phone rang. Winter.

"Missed me already, big guy?"

"Your diviner's here. He's had a terrible vision but won't talk about it until you get back."

"Put Faion on the phone."

"*Hey, short stack,*" Faion said. "*Better get here. Winter's got zero chill.*"

"You had a vision?"

"*Yes, and Gran confirmed my fears. Supernatural creatures are gathering in the empty spaces in-between the realms, preparing to fight.*"

"The realms? Which ones?"

Faion sounded frantic. "*Every damn one.*"

All five realms? There were thousands of gates connecting the Deep Down, the Shadow Realm, the Eternal Halls, the exile vortex and the basic world. A war with a thousand fronts is an impossible war.

"Stay put," I said. "You can trust Winter, Faion, give him a full account and I will be there soon."

I hurried into the 7-Eleven and found Carter chatting with a young guy who was stocking the soda fridges.

"We have to go," I said.

"Okay, one second."

"Now, Carter."

Carter huffed but followed me. "I haven't even grabbed my Monsters yet. He was in the process of putting them on the shelf."

"Sorry, but this can't wait."

Carter studied my face as we ducked into the car. "What's happening?"

"Monsters," I told him. "The real kind. About to be put in the world."

WE RAN TO WINTER'S door. Faion jumped to his feet when we entered.

"When did it start?" I asked.

"Don't know," he said. "A while. Gran said Horpheus dispatched scouts. They reported that paranormal fields are swelling, but the beasts are waiting for something, a signal maybe, before they break through the portals."

What are they waiting for? If Horror had orchestrated everything, then the creatures were waiting on me. It could be another one of his tests. *Either I choose him, or I die in defense of the realms.* Either way, the question would have been answered and he wouldn't have to kill me directly.

"What do we need?" Winter said.

"Everyone. We need everyone and everything."

Winter started for the bedroom. "I'll call Kirsi. She'll bring the Valkyries."

The Valkyries always came. They were the best of us. I knew they were still mourning the sister who was lost the last time they came to our aid.

"Faion," Carter said. "Do we know which portals to defend?"

"Yeah," Faion said. "Every damn one. Same as I told Luna."

"I didn't think she actually meant *every* portal when she told me that."

"That girl says what she means. Believe that," Faion said. "If there's a portal, then there's a horde of fabled monstrosities behind it." He reached an open hand out to Carter. "If you have a spare sword, I'll put it to use."

Oh no, I said we needed *everyone*.

"Your honor inspires us, my friend," I said, "but you would not survive riding the ley lines."

Faion's eyes widened. "You been riding ley line currents?"

"The perks of immortality," Carter said.

"That's top bitch power moves right there," Faion said.

"Message sent," Winter said returning from the bedroom. He noticed my uncertainty. "What's on your mind?"

"I'm thinking... I don't know. This might finally be it," I said. "The war for the five realms. It's always been this thing that was coming in the far-away future, but now it's different. It's here. And there's nothing out there in the future anymore, nothing beyond now."

The room fell silent. Everyone looked at each other, then inward.

Winter inhaled deeply. "It'll have to be written then."

WE WERE DRESSED TO kill. Literally. Armed with enchanted blades, crossbows and arrows, we wore heavy leather armors secured by tight strings and combat boots, as Carter called them. The ensemble was designed for full-out battle and made us look like lobsters on steroids, but in fact the enchanted leather used for the armor felt light as a feather and allowed for full freedom of movement.

The ley line express reached the final stop, launching us forward until we landed on something soft and cushiony. I realized it was hay. We had landed outside a hay barn somewhere in northern Wisconsin. I felt like it had taken us mere minutes to get here from Southern California, but ley line currents distorted perception of time. Faion had sensed the densest paranormal activity near this portal in the upper Midwest.

A sudden, irrational fear raced through my mind. What if Winter wasn't yet strong enough for ley line travel? What if he had used too much of his energy to heal and escape his imprisonment? Or worse, what if Horror was the source of Winter's sudden recovery and then reversed it to leave his core weakened to face the dangers he knew would come?

Winter felt my eyes on him. "Do I have snot on my face?"

"No," I said. "You look perfect. You'd tell me if you didn't feel one hundred percent, right? You are just getting back on your feet."

Carter motioned us to be quiet. He knelt and felt the ground with his fingertips. "Three different scents," he said.

"Maybe two hours old."

Winter flared his nostrils. "I feel it, too. Unidentifiable essences. The scent trail leads to the portal."

Shadows had impeccable senses. If Winter couldn't discern what those etheric essences were, it meant they were extremely uncommon.

We moved forward. The portal should be nearby. We could see only an open field of clover stretching before us.

Carter tapped a patch of grass with his boot. "Here," he said.

I stared at the grass. "Where?"

Carter kicked aside the grass patch to reveal a three-foot-wide opening.

The gap contained a bottomless darkness.

"That's the portal?" I said.

"Not quite, the portal is at the bottom," Winter clarified.

I furrowed my brow. "I don't see a bottom."

"Exactly," he said.

Suddenly, my stomach constricted. I got a very bad feeling. I really didn't want to jump into a black hole. What if there was a burning fire at the bottom, or what if we fell forever?

"I'll go first," Carter said.

I opened my mouth to protest, but he was already gone.

"You're next," Winter said. He noticed my hesitation. "It's just a portal. Carter's on the other side. Don't worry."

I fixed him with a pleading stare. "Promise me you'll be right behind."

"Of course."

I took a deep breath and prepared myself for the leap into the bottomless pit.

Winter pulled me back, spun me into his arms and kissed me.

"In case we don't make it out," he said.

I stared at him, dumbfounded.

He laughed. "Just messing with you."

I am not amused.

"Go," he said, "I'll see you on the other side."

"You're doing it again…"

He turned me back around and nudged me over the edge.

As I fell into the dark pit, gravity pushed my intestines into my throat. Liquid skipped off my skin and clothes as I kept falling rapidly. My feet punched through something gooey. I immediately felt weightless as I continued falling. I shivered before spotting a flickering light ahead.

At that same moment, I crashed into Carter.

"Get clear," he said.

He grabbed my arm, then pushed me between my shoulder blades. We rolled onto a rough, wet ground. Winter landed with a thud right next to us. If Carter hadn't pushed me out of the way, Winter's dense, muscled body would have crushed me like a soda can.

My butt hurt. Carter pulled me up onto my feet. We were in a tunnel. It should have been pitch black, but a pale energy field flickered above, likely fueled by portal energy. My eyes adjusted to the dim glow.

"Let's keep moving," Winter said.

We walked the tunnel. The ground was slick. The odor of stale air hit my nostrils. Odd-looking vines grew on the wet walls like thick green veins.

The tunnel turned sharply. The portal hissed with electricity. A black whirlpool of energy hummed at its core.

I braced myself for the impact. We jumped through the portal as one. The current stung like tiny needles peeling back layers of skin.

We were thrust into a wide cavern lit by crisscrossing energy beams.

"Let's never do that again," I said, checking my face to make sure I still had flesh.

"We were promised hordes of monsters," Carter said. "Where are they?"

Valid question. We had reached the vacant space between the basic world and the Deep Down, where Faion's divining powers had sensed creatures and the scouts of Horpheus had confirmed swollen paranormal fields, yet there was not so much as a church mouse stirring.

Winter waved his hand in front of him. "Something's off," he said.

I felt it too. Not only were there no signs of mythic monsters, but the energy coming out of Carter and Winter felt off. I couldn't quite pinpoint what was wrong with their etheric essences except that it felt like they had gone.

A metal gate materialized out of nowhere. It slowly slid open, baiting us to enter. A crazy thought formed. If I could just seal the gate, we could trap the monsters. It made no sense, but I kept repeating it to myself like a mantra. *Seal those gates with the strongest of spells, then run the other way.*

Flames exploded behind the gate. The metal turned a crimson red as the blaze burst higher. A scorching air current rushed over us, like a giant hot oven just opened. The temperature rose fast. I couldn't breathe.

My mind reeled with images of my lung tissue burning like paper as I gasped and choked for air.

I backed away. Whatever was happening, I wanted none of it.

My ears buzzed. Strange words flooded my brain... *areika, herrat, ignitius, pyrrha.*

Winter's body brushed against mine from behind, and I leaned into him, my back arching against his powerful torso. He said something, I knew he did, but I couldn't understand.

The enchanted words kept resonating in my head. The fire was the result of a powerful spell as old as time, and those same words that kept feeding it into existence were swimming in my blood, inviting me to use them.

In a daze, I repeated the fire spell in my mind, slowly, assuredly. The flames responded, shrinking down. It dawned on me that I could dominate the spell, that I could diminish the flames with sheer willpower.

Winter wrapped his arms around me. I tried to pull away, but it was too late. The flames raged again. Winter picked me up like I was made of feathers and handed me to Carter.

My squire backed up, one hand under my neck, the other under my knees. Winter crouched. I tried to protest but nobody paid me any attention. Carter ran at Winter, stepped onto his back and used it as a springboard. We shot up over the flames and landed behind the gate. Winter landed next to us.

Whoa! Those flames were twenty feet high. The physical capabilities of Immortals never ceased to amaze.

Carter set me on my feet. The flames flickered down and died.

Did we pass Horror's test?

Winter looked me over carefully. "The fire paralyzed you."

"I hate fire spells with a vengeance," I said, "but there was something else. It was as if the spell spoke to me."

The moment I said it, I realized how it sounded. Crazy.

"Faion's antennae were a mile off," Carter said. "There's nothing here."

A shudder scampered down my spine. "No, there's something." I reached out and touched the wall. My hand recoiled at the feeling of dense, dark magic streaming down the walls, its reverberations slithering through the air like translucent eels.

"Yes, and it's fueling this paranormal invasion," Winter said. "Some strange and powerful and terrible thing."

"Horror," I muttered under my breath.

"Could be," Winter said. "The magic is ancient."

The walls and the ceiling bulged wider, then shrank back, like a bubble bursting. Supernatural creatures finally spilled out of the walls, crawling along the ground like an army of huge lizards with sharp talons and birdlike beaks.

What cursed reptiles are these?

Once they all hit the floor, they stood upright. Most of them reached about three feet in height, but a few were taller.

We backed up, slowly.

"Savroids," Winter said.

"Savroids?" I repeated. "What in holy hell?"

"If hell existed, it wouldn't have them," Carter said. "Lizard people who feed on human flesh are not supposed to exist. It's a fable, a scary story Immortals tell their children when they misbehave."

"They're right there," Winter said. "I knew they were real when I was a child. My mother took me to an Etruscan village they had massacred. Soon after, they were banished. If it comes to it, we'll cut them down easily. They're intelligent, but they don't possess magic."

Intelligent lizard people who eat humans, charming.

The Savroids stared and snapped their beaks, waiting for their moment.

A Savroid spat out a massive fireball. Carter pulled his sword out and swatted the fireball straight back at the Savroid. The fireball came apart and collided against an invisible wall, fizzling out with a loud pop.

"A fucking energy shield," Winter said.

No magic, huh?

For a split second, my eyes met Winter's. Then he ran off into the fray. The creatures immediately circled him.

Carter charged after Winter. He kicked a Savroid in the gut, launching it into the ceiling like a missile. Another Savroid fell at my feet. Instinctively, I stomped its head. I'd hoped we'd find a way to force the creatures back into their banished world, but there was no such portal in sight.

Carter and Winter worked methodically, switching between carving hides with their blades and literally kicking ass with their feet.

A group of Savroids splintered away from the others to rush me as one. I acted quickly, working up a force field to hurl at them. A few were caught in the whirlwind of my lethal energy, but the rest sheltered within a thick energy shield. I struck again while the shield still sizzled red from my previous assault. The shield held solid. I somehow gathered more power from my cells and the shield finally cracked. The Savroids tried to regroup and charge me one last time, but they weren't fast enough. My energy field swept them off their feet and flung them against the hard wall.

The wall absorbed them with a swoosh.

Wait, is there a portal inside the wall?

Winter roared out of the darkness. The walls shuddered. "Aim for the abdomen!"

He towered over me, a six-foot-two collection of hard muscle and monomaniacal badassery. Across his left forearm, a wound that exposed bone and muscle healed rapidly. His regenerative powers were just fine.

"You alright?" he yelled, exploding teeth out of a Savroid's mouth with a crushing blow from his sword's hilt.

"Same shit, different day," I yelled back. "Good cardio though!"

The fact that we were joking meant it was a little too easy. The Savroids were dangerous and lethal. They would cause great harm to basic humans, but to the three of us, they were little more than a swarm of mosquitos.

I hurled a lightning bolt at a new horde of Savroids. The bolt cut into their shields like a spoon in jelly. Their hides instantly blistered, causing them to fall to the ground convulsing.

Winter tore a Savroid's arm off with his bare hands.

Eek!

"Use my sword," Winter shouted. "You have it for a reason. You need to get some practice."

I swirled on my feet and released an electric current that cut clean through the midsection of three Savroids. "I'm good, thanks. I'm not a Neanderthal. I'll stick to my magic."

"Let her be," Carter yelled. "She's too stubborn and untrainable. It's a lot easier just to kill a thousand of these nasty things."

Oh my god, those two are the worst and not funny.

An earsplitting thud rolled through the cave like the crack of lightning. The Savroids cowered against the walls, whimpering. A ten-foot-tall Savroid punched its way through the far wall of the cave. It stood on a pile of debris on two powerful legs. Its head was huge. Sharp teeth protruded from its half open beak. Its eyes were a sick orange. Its arms were coiled in blue flames. It wore a tight golden dog collar around its neck.

Its beak opened wide. "Now you die in agony."

Holy shit! It spoke. His voice was a deep rasp, his diction completely lacked clarity, but his intent was quite unmistakable.

The Savroid raised his blazing arms. He began chanting. Waves of intense heat shot out of him like lava gusts. The cave became a scorching oven. Sweat ran down my face. It felt like falling into an active volcano.

Carter charged the Savroid. He was met with oodles of magic. His blade melted before he reached his target. Carter tossed the sword aside, pain bending his features. His palm was blistered flesh.

Big ouch!

I scoffed. "So much for your precious swords."

A purple whirlwind formed in my palm. I hit the Savroid with mega volts of energy that would have barbecued a T-rex on the spot. Instead, it zapped right off his shield and exploded against the ceiling.

A rocky avalanche rained down, burying many of the smaller Savroids.

Some good at least.

I spat dirt out of my mouth. The huge bastard resumed chanting. In front of our eyes, something translucent materialized: a portal to the basic world.

Fucking fuck!

I closed my eyes to concentrate all the energy I had left onto his shield. When I squeezed the energy tighter and tighter, a phosphorescent green light funneled out of me like a freight train, attacking everything in sight except for Carter and Winter. I must have subconsciously encased the Immortals inside a blue shield while consciously cooking up an assault.

The few Savroid survivors fell, clutching their stomachs, but their alpha's shield held.

Winter quickly stripped down. His body tensed, his muscles readied to spring him forward. He lifted his head and roared like a possessed beast.

Oh my.

He charged the shield, leaping high to land a blow from above. Magic thundered and Winter rolled off the shield, his scorched skin smoking with flesh fumes.

Winter landed and snorted, then began a long exhale to cool down his ravaged skin enough for the healing to begin. He sprinted into the Savroid's shield again. The crashing impact knocked Winter back.

The Savroid chanted faster. The portal solidified.

Winter shook off the smoke from his arms and rammed the shield one more time. The energy holding the shield in place gave way. Winter burst through it, his entire body in flames.

Oh lord. I glanced at Carter with pleading eyes.

Carter shook his head. "Trust him."

Winter leaped at the Savroid and grasped him with fire hands. They clashed and collided with the rock wall. Winter clamped his arms around the giant Savroid's abdomen and lifted it off the ground. Muscles bulged under Winter's shredded skin. Fury raged in the Savroid's eyes. Winter squeezed harder, tossed the creature into the air like a giant ragdoll, caught it by its head on the way down and then spun in a manner that ripped the beast's head clean off.

Blood gushed from the stump of the neck, drenching Winter in a fountain of dark crimson.

Any Savroid still whimpering on the ground vanished, pulled into the invisible time portal inside the wall, one after the other.

The dead remained.

We ran to Winter. His body was coated in Savroid blood; third-degree burns bubbled out as the blood slid off him. I tried to hug him, but he writhed in pain.

"Air hug," he moaned.

"You silly fool," I said, laughing.

I did it. I gave him an air hug, but I also found a place

on his forehead where my lips could make it to the crazy man's bloody skin and plant a long, gentle kiss that I hoped, somehow, would help him heal.

Chapter 16

Dragging myself to the shower was a cruel torment. I had healed from the ugly injuries of the battle, but I still ached all over. Winter left in the middle of the night to meet with the Valkyries who had encountered more Savroids in the Florida Keys. Watching him tear the giant's head off with his bare hands was disturbing enough, but him running straight to the aftermath of another battle with barely two hours of sleep spiked my anxiety.

Mixing copious amounts of red wine and watching Squid Game until the wee hours proved to be a bad cocktail. My reward this morning was a manic monkey brain that wouldn't relax for a second.

Horror needed to get out of my head. He anchored my every thought and it left me feeling helpless.

Was it his dark magic I sensed inside the tunnels? Could he ever be trusted in the least? Would he stop at nothing to achieve complete dominion?

Walking through a sea of Winter's shirts and sweaters in his closet did nothing to ease my nerves. After an hour, I stopped pretending I could get my anxiety under control staying in the condo. I needed a break from all my worries. I needed to think about anything else.

Lily had been the place I went to reset since we met five years ago. I walked the beach, waiting for her to answer my call.

"*What happened*?" she said with a hint of accusation.

"Hello to you, too," I said into the phone. "I'll tell you over lunch?"

"*Yeah, you will. Let's do a 12:30,*" she said slowly. "*I'm at the bank with Lucia. She's finally taking out a loan for her bakery.*"

"How about now?"

"*I knew it. Drama alert. It's not even ten, Sophie. Something juicy and wicked has happened. I can feel it.*"

Almost exactly right. Definitely something wicked and, unfortunately, a whole bunch of juicy bits of guts and gore and smashed brains.

"Can you steal away for an hour?" I said.

"*Oh, you messy girl, but of course. Meet me at Café Sevilla. They make a mean chorizo paella.*"

"All you think about is food."

"*Food's my boyfriend,*" she said. Hard not to love her.

My Uber dropped me off outside Café Sevilla within

twenty minutes. I'd been rehearsing how to tell Lily that I had broken up with Cyrus.

She sat scrolling on her phone in the waiting area inside. She popped up to give me a kiss on the cheek and a warm smile, but as soon as we sat down, she was ready for some gossip.

"I need it all," Lily said. "Every possible detail about your wedding rehearsal."

"Kill me first," I said. "That would be more enjoyable."

She reached out to touch my unkempt hair. She considered my clothes and my general state with clear disapproval. "You look like you pulled a double shift at a Tijuana brothel."

"A charming way to put it," I said, rubbing my temples.

"Is it a headache or a cry for help? Wait, are you pregnant?"

I'd have to have sex first.

"It's a pounding headache, Lil."

"*Pounding*, huh? Freud would now ask if your rambunctious fiancé went thump in the night?"

Oh, boy.

"About that..." I started to say.

Lily looked disgusted. "No, don't tell me. Are you about to say you haven't slept with him yet? Sophie, seriously, you need to get laid before they come and take Miss Marvelous away from you for neglect. No wonder you have a headache. You're all backed up."

"Not sure women get backed up," I said.

"Really? Because I'm looking at such a woman right now."

The waiter appeared magically as if on cue. He was cute, but his lips were pursed together like mirth was his enemy.

"Two caffè lattes," Lily told him. "And tell Paco to cook me up a chorizo paella. Oh, and a slice of cake. Chocolate. She's going to need it."

"I'm sorry, miss. We don't have paella on the breakfast menu."

Lily stared up into his piercing brown eyes. "I'm an *off the menu* kind of girl. Tell Paco. He'll know exactly who it's for."

The waiter stared at her, curiously, before nodding and disappearing.

"He's young, but he's kind of sizzle hot," Lily said.

"Maybe it's time you do more than rate every man you see," I said. Turning the tables on her seemed like a good idea.

Lily landed her eyes on mine like a slap. "There isn't a man on Earth that deserves this little treasure. And don't change the subject. What manner of mistakes were made at your wedding rehearsal? Were they messy?"

Ugh, tell her, just tell her. Get it out of the way.

"You could say that. Cyrus and I... we decided to call it quits."

She lifted her eyebrows in disbelief. "You need to slow your roll, Sophie. Wind it back and start from the beginning."

I exhaled. "It began with a mutual decision, and it honestly didn't come as a surprise. The whole thing was rushed and stupid."

"The whole thing?" she said. "So, it's not just the wedding?"

"Yeah," I said. "Cyrus being Cyrus, it was an all or nothing kind of thing. That's how we got to the premature engagement to begin with."

"Poor Sophie, a hot, loaded guy wanted to give you the princess fit."

"It didn't fit," I said. "That whole life. It's not me. As much as he looks at himself in the mirror, he can be his own princess."

Lily looked confused. "I was thinking it didn't fit you, not even a little, so... why did you get engaged again?"

"One of us has to try," I said. "At least I date."

"I date," she said, mildly offended. "I just don't second-date."

"Half hooking up just to be unimpressed doesn't qualify as dating. I don't have the energy to dive into your delusions right now but stick a pin in it, sis. We're most def coming back to this when I can get the fucking hamster wheel to stop spinning in my head."

"I would totally second-date the right guy," she said.

"Yeah, when he exists, you mean."

"You're dumb."

"Sick burn."

I was finally grinning when the waiter brought our caffè lattes.

"You have no idea how much Lucia was looking forward to baking that cake and meeting your mystery man. And your poor Grandma. How will she take the news? She didn't even get to meet this short-term fiancé."

"Well, since she tells every person I introduce her to the story of how I fell into the fishpond on graduation day, I guess I dodged a bullet."

"A classic Collinsworth," Lily said with a chuckle. "Your skirt rose to the surface and those sheer panties were totally see-through when wet. Good thing I suggested we get Brazilians the day before."

I gave her a stern look. "Why is it that every time I embarrass myself you call it a *classic Collinsworth*?"

"That a serious question? Soph, it's your brand."

Slurping my latte, I shook my head. "Bad friend."

"Nonsense, I'm your best friend. I happen to think you're adorable when you're embarrassed. You glow."

"One chorizo paella and a slice of chocolate cake," the waiter said, glancing down at me.

Lily grabbed his forearm. "Could you help us?"

Our strapping young waiter seemed lost for a second. He cleared his throat as Lily slowly released his arm. "Of course. What can I do?"

"What do you think of my friend?" Lily said, pointing to

me. "Do you think any man would be wise to hold onto her?"

What the fuck, Lil?

He hesitated, considering the situation. *Poor guy.* When he finally arrived at an answer, he unleashed a toothy smile. I wanted to slide under the table.

"Absolutely," he said, winking at me.

"Thanks, sweetie," Lily said triumphantly.

He grinned again. "Anything else, ladies?"

"No. We're all good in the hood," Lily said.

Yet another waiter mesmerized by Lily.

"See?" she said as soon as the waiter was gone.

"That was awkward," I said under my breath. "I see a waiter looking for a tip and maybe your phone number. Not mine."

"My God, Soph! Did you even see the way he looked at you?"

"You literally made him look at me."

"Okay, but he'd been wanting to stare at you. I just helped."

"My ego is fine," I said. "I don't need you to frighten men for me."

"Oh, I do that for me," she said. "It's quite fun. I just need my girl to remember what Cyrus saw in you. A little brilliant sexpot. The way he looked at you is the way every woman wants to be looked at."

"Just eat your paella, food slut," I said, sipping my coffee.

"It's not slutty if I'm in love," she said and then took a monster bite.

WE WALKED TO LILY'S car in the underground parking garage.

"Do you want me to drop you at your place?" Lily said as she took the keys out of her purse.

I hadn't told her I'd moved in with Winter. I knew she said she'd never judge but telling her I'd moved in with another man only hours after I cancelled my wedding... Well, that would just make her worry.

"Drop me on campus, near the library," I said.

Something growled nearby—a long, wailing sound like a wounded lion. I spun around, my senses at peak alert.

The overhead lights flickered and sizzled.

Lily grabbed my hand. "What's happening?"

"Lil, get in the car and drive away," I said, my eyes fixed on a support column at the far end of the parking garage.

"What? Are you nuts?" Lily said. "I'm not leaving you."

Metal clanked on cement. My eyes searched until a creature stepped out from behind a cement support column.

A chill ran through me. A five-foot-tall Savroid walked upright towards us on two wobbling legs. Its slick black body was spotted with red blotches. Its beak was long and sharp. It glared its amber eyes.

Lily screamed.

Poor girl. I can't imagine what she's thinking.

I scanned the parking garage. Just Lily, me and the other-worldly beast.

The Savroid roared. Saliva drooled onto its chest. Its savage essence could be felt pulsing in the air.

Lily screamed louder and more terrified. I yanked the car door open and pushed her inside. "It will be fine," I told her before slamming the door shut, fusing all four locks with a jolt of energy.

Sorry, Lily. I don't know what else to do.

The Savroid would have to go through me to get to her. Not happening.

I walked away from the car, searching for the closest ley line. Lily banged on the locked doors, trying the handles. Her panic became muffled as I focused in on the eternal powers of the universe.

I pulled my magic close. My hands sparked up a golden current.

My turn to glare at the Savroid. "You want me? Come and get me."

The monster took a step forward and snapped its beak. Two huge black wings unfolded behind its shoulders.

Fucking hell.

The Savroid took another step. Every time its talons touched the ground, orange sparks crackled on the pavement.

Nice trick.

Strong, destroyer magic was out of the question. I couldn't zap the Savroid to bloody chunks, not with Lily in the front seat of this drive-in from hell in the bustling heart of the city. Cars and phone cams could drive by at any moment, and I didn't have Horror here to erase memories.

The Savroid's eyes narrowed. It unfurled its wings, took a running start and charged, accelerating with each step. My shield was already in place and waiting to fry the beast when it made contact.

The Savroid sprinted the last few feet, jumped and glided over my head to land heavily on the roof of Lily's car.

The talons hammered the car with rapid blows. Lily squirmed frantically in the car as the talons punctured the roof, nearly stabbing her.

Shit, shit, shit!

Fury filled my lungs. I stood my ground and called onto all my elemental magic. A swirling cyclone of leaves, branches and dust raced down the ramp like an avalanche.

The Savroid was caught up in the whirlwind, swept off the car and smashed viciously against the ceiling of the lot.

It shook its head, staggered for a moment and then swooped at me, black wings flapping, talons positioned to shred.

I dived forward and slid under the monster. I spun onto my back to create an enormous magnetic field and hurled it at the Savroid like a net, trapping the horrid beast inside.

The energy hugged tighter so the creature could barely move. Its eyes filled with murderous rage. A fireball shot from its beak and splatted against the magnetic field.

I increased the intensity of the force. The creature clung onto the field with claws and talons, trying to tear it open. The force field zapped the Savroid again and again, energy ripping through its core. The creature let out a bloodcurdling yelp.

With a twist of my right hand, I lifted the magnetic field off the ground with the Savroid inside. With my other hand, I created a chain of energy rings to activate the hidden time portal.

No matter how hard the Savroid tried to break free, my force field did not yield, overpowering and injuring the beast with each attempt.

When the portal cracked open, I edged all my magnetic energy in the crack until the Savroid was sucked into the time portal. In the final moment, his features became even more grotesque. A circle of fire formed around the portal and popped. It was gone like it had never been.

I climbed onto my feet using a support column to steady myself. I tried to catch my breath. My hands trembled and I sweated profusely.

The realization of what had happened kicked in. The dark forces in the portal tunnels had imprinted on me. The Savroid had followed me here.

Nails scratched against glass.

Lily.

She had witnessed my power. My heart sank. My one true basic friend who kept me sane and grounded had witnessed the dark, vicious side of me. Our friendship would be forever changed, if it survived at all.

As long as she stayed safe, I could handle anything.

I limped to the car and unfused the door locks. Lily stared at me like she didn't recognize me. Her eyes were still frantic. Salty streaks stained her cheeks. She swayed when she breathed, having hyperventilated.

Not knowing what to do, I tried to hug her. She shoved me aside, jumped out of the car and ran clumsily to where the portal had vanished.

Her upper body kept shaking.

I went to her. "Lily, it's okay. You're safe now."

Her eyes filled with tears. This was no longer my self-assured Lily.

"Talk to me," I said softly.

"A beast from my fucking nightmares, a fucking terrible, unnatural fucking terrifying fucking beast tried to kill us," she said. "And you were doing whatever you were and..." Her whole body tensed. Her lips trembled. "What the hell are you, Sophie?"

I stared at her at a loss for words. In some ways what I was, what I truly was, was finally hitting me for the first time as well. It had never felt completely real until Lily looked at me with those frightened, unloving eyes.

"I'll explain everything, I promise," I said, my gaze dropping in defeat.

Lily stumbled. I raised my head in time to see her eyes roll back in their sockets. Her knees buckled. I lunged in time to catch her before she collapsed.

Holding her in my arms, I managed to get my phone out. It took a few tries before I could find Emmet's number.

"I didn't know who else to call," I said when I heard his voice. "Lily needs you." I started sobbing. "We both need you."

Chapter 17

I WAITED ACROSS THE street from Lucia's house for half an hour before Emmet walked out. His face was hard to read. He took my arm and led me to a bench.

"How is Lily?" I said.

"Physically? She's fine. Emotionally? That's a whole different story. How could you let her see so much, Sophie?"

"It all happened so fast. We just ate and were walking to Lily's car in the ramp and then the beast attacked out of nowhere. It came from a time portal and then he jumped me and landed on Lily's car with her in it. You saw the car. I thought she'd be killed. I found a way to use elemental energy to blast the beast back into the portal. I didn't have time to think, Emmet."

"Jesus. And Lily saw all that?"

I nodded.

"That's rough," Emmet said.

That's putting it mildly. Lily probably questioned everything in her life right now.

"What have you told her?" I said.

"Not much. I told her everything's okay. Sophie is still Sophie, and that I would talk to you to get this all figured out."

"Will we?"

"Whatever happens, you're not going to lose Lily or me."

"I trust you. Tell her everything. Whatever you think you should. Tell her about the hidden realms. Tell her we're both a part of a supernatural world."

"I'll take it slow," he said. "See how she responds."

"Thank you. You are a true friend. Spare her our details for now. Don't do anything crazy like shifting in front of her. She's not ready for all that. Most of all, tell her I'm sorry and I love her very much."

Emmet frowned. "Maybe it should be you telling her that."

"Don't tell her this, but there are people I have to warn. I can't let emotions get the better of me. This is not good, Emmet. Everything hangs in the balance. A cruel, long war is beginning."

He sighed heavily. "Cyrus says the same thing. By the way, he's been intolerable since you two fell out. He wanders around the Keep like a broken man, barking out half-hearted orders that make no sense. He's depressing everyone. His own security hide from his view whenever they can."

I raised my hand to stop him. "I don't want to hear about Cyrus. He's not who you think he is. He's manipulative and dangerous. Please, stay away from him. In fact, his security has the right idea, put as much distance between you and him as possible. Terrible days are upon us. I don't want you caught on the wrong side."

He knew everything I was saying, but I needed him to know he had friends outside the pack who also cared about him.

"And how about you, Sophie? The darkness seems to follow you."

"My name's Luna," I said. "I'm supposed to be the light in the dark. If I could run, I would, but with my essence, there's nowhere to hide."

"And I am your friend," he said. "I'm supposed to be there when you call. You have many who love you. Don't forget that. You are not alone."

"Can you stay with Lil and make sure she's safe?"

I swallowed down a sob. It was becoming clear that for all my power, I could not always protect those closest to me. Lily, Gram, Faion, they all had targets on their backs.

"That's already on lock," Emmet said. "I won't let her out of my sight. You can cross that concern off your worry list."

I hugged him tight. He always smelled so good. "I realize we have a lopsided friendship. Thank you, Emmet."

He smiled. "Are you kidding? You provide ninety percent of my adrenaline rushes. You're like a permanent skydive."

"Right, but without a parachute."

"Exactly," he said.

"You're sweet, but a bad liar," I teased him. "Now go protect our girl."

Emmet crossed the street and vanished into Lucia's house. I hoped his natural kindness would help Lily process all the trauma she had just survived.

I dropped my head and sighed. "You can show your face."

Chaos jumped from a pine tree and landed softly like a jungle cat sniffing out nearby prey.

"It was hard not to projectile vomit listening to a conversation between two greeting cards," he said. "I thought wolfie would never prance off."

I grabbed him by his coat collar and dragged him away. "Don't be jealous of those with actual hearts, you cold bastard."

"Have you had Bison heart tacos? They're quite good."

"Never mind that, you sensed it, didn't you?"

"If by *sensed it* you mean the mingling of your essence with a beast's essence in an aggressive stand-off? Yeah, cupcake, I did."

"That means Horror sensed it as well," I said.

"Most certainly."

"See, that concerns me. He has the annoying habit of popping into my head to chat me up when I'm in deep trouble. But not this time."

"Are you suggesting that our dear old Dad could be

behind all of this beast business?" Chaos said.

"The thought has crossed my mind."

"Not sure it matches his style."

"He has a style?"

"Call it obsessive compulsive. He likes his rituals to which he rarely goes astray. Precisely what happened?"

I laid out the whole Savroid saga for him. As he listened, his face went from curious to pale to red rage.

"It's our cue to make ourselves scarce," he said. "Bora Bora is lovely this time of the year. Any time, really."

He's so predictable.

"You want to run? Again? You're not serious."

"Quite serious. Horror is never far. He has spies every-where by now. The only reason he hasn't come for us is he's not entirely certain he can take on both of us. Soon he will arrive at the certainty. He grows stronger by the day."

I studied my brother's face. "He likes to call you a coward, but I know that's the last thing you are. Why does he unnerve you so? Your first instinct is always to run."

He grabbed my shoulders. "I'm a pragmatist, lesser sibling. I won't engage in a fight I know I can't win. There is a hidden portal in Bora Bora he doesn't know about. I'm the only one alive who knows. We could cross to the other side and throw away the proverbial key, so to speak. It's a forgotten paradise. Used to be a fairy kingdom. We could stay hidden for decades or centuries."

"Or millennia," I said, rolling my eyes.

"If that's what it takes," he said, stubbornly.

"I'm sorry, I won't run from this. My best friend was attacked today. She might never be the same. I have people to protect."

He grabbed my arm and shoved me against a jacaranda tree. His eyes were on fire. "You don't want to leave that icy prick who shares your bed. That's it, isn't it? You'll risk your immortal life for that dullard."

I zapped his hand with a sharp blast. He pulled away in pain.

"Get real," I yelled at him. "You yourself went to great trouble to save Winter. And I refuse to be your punching bag. Get rough with me again and you'll lose more than your hand."

The anger drained from his face. "A prophecy has long been told, reckless waif, that the offspring of the dark one will take from him his eternal life, but prophecies are possibilities, not things written in stone. Have foresight, sister, visualize a bigger picture. Time is our biggest ally."

There was a sad fatigue in his voice. It occurred to me that I didn't want to let him down. If it was a manipulation tactic, it was working.

"Horror gifted me the vanishing smoke," I said. "Or so he said."

Chaos's eyebrows came together. "You have the power of portal traveling, and you haven't bothered to test it? You are a complete bore."

"I don't want anything from him."

Chaos shook his head. "You are thick. Even the old bastard is wanting you to sit this one out, Luna."

And if we beat Horror at his own game, what then? Would Chaos claim our father's forbidden powers and domain? Was that the plan? As much as I would like to, I couldn't dismiss the possibility that Chaos wanted the same absolute power Horror wanted.

Blue smoke sheathed Chaos's hand, creeping up his arm, flowing out of him like it was steam.

"The blue smoke runs in our blood," he said. "And if you manage to get some of that icy dullard's blood inside your own bloodstream, you'll be able to find him through the smoke whenever you want."

Nice tip. Right. Somehow convince Winter to mix his blood with mine so he can kiss all his privacy goodbye.

"Just something to think about, moon kitty," Chaos said. "Don't forget what I said about Bora Bora. If you have to, use your schoolgirl charms to get the melting snowman to join us."

The smoke cloaked his torso and legs, and Chaos was gone.

He didn't get it. He never would.

A blue light reemerged in the very spot where Chaos had stood before vanishing. A tendril of the smoke he'd left behind dashed along the path to lick my feet. Magic ebbed and flowed along my skin, sharp like nails. A wall of thick blue mist rose and covered my face, sealing me off from the world around me.

The ground I stood on cracked. Power pooled under my feet, propelling me upwards. It burst through my body like a piercing current of pain, lighting my magic core on fire.

Anguish ripped through me. I screamed as I wafted within a blue light so bright I could barely see. When I had teleported with Chaos before, he had protected me from the energy assault, but now I was fully exposed to the raw power of my own blood like a defenseless infant.

Every cell in my body ached with a stinging agony. My body swirled inside a vicious cyclone. Finally, the hallucinating trip slowed down. I crashed down inside Winter's condo with a cracking thunder. My body felt like I was floating, rubbery and tattered. A transparent layer of energy kept me floating above the floor and the furniture, suspended inside the cobalt smoke, caught in a place between places.

Through a thin veil of vapor, unseen and undetected, I watched a woman walk out of the kitchen carrying a coffee cup. A familiar, attractive face and a fit body in tight leather pants.

Winter followed Chazona into the room. Good, he was in one piece.

I saw them clearly. They started talking in front of the window, looking all cozy and fuzzy.

Those are really tight pants.

Chazona wouldn't miss a single opportunity to stalk him

and keep an eye on him. The ice queen was doing damage control. I hated the flood of petty thoughts in my head. Why did he give her the benefit of the doubt after all the crap she had pulled? My blood boiled and I couldn't stop it.

Their backs were to me, but their body language told me they'd been discussing something important.

"The Grand Magistrate is willing to overlook the events of the past year," Chazona said. "Come back to the council, Winter. Claim your legacy. You are meant for greatness. Don't throw it all away."

I noticed she avoided labeling me an awful influence. *Smart move.*

"My mind's made up," Winter said. "Watch your back, Chaz. There are more weasels than knights on the council."

Chazona nodded agreeably. She spun an animated tale to my tired boyfriend about how wonderful it would be for everything to go back to the way things used to be. He seemed interested in all that Miss Sexy Leather Pants had to say.

Winter spun around. His eyes grew intense. "Darius will not yield. He will not go gentle into that good night. And if not him, then Horror will come knocking. Our world will not be safe until we wipe away every trace of his vile bloodline."

A hidden knife cut through my stomach. If I told him that Horror's vile blood ran through my veins, would I, too, be wiped away?

Chazona leaned snugly on him from behind. Her arms wrapped tightly around his waist. "If that's what it takes to get you to come back, then that's what we'll do. We'll wipe Horror's bloodline off the face of the planet."

Winter's smile was labored. "Easier said than done."

Ugh, Winter, she's playing you, snap out of it.

I was tempted to jump out of my protective cocoon to slap some sense into him. I realized he saw what he needed to see. In that moment, I knew I could never bring myself to tell him Helen and Christian had been murdered, or that Chazona was one of the responsible parties.

He trusted that woman. He would lose control if he knew the depths of her deceit. I would be signing her death warrant and, at the same time, putting Winter at risk. I was still haunted from watching Winter kill Dimitri, an Immortal Magistrate, to keep me safe. I didn't want to imagine what he would do to Chazona.

I didn't want her dead, I just wanted to cut her tongue out and maybe buy her some loose-fitting slacks.

Chapter 18

IT TOOK ME A while to recalibrate the blue smoke destination. I wanted to end up outside the condo instead of inside. I waited until Chazona left. I had no wish to talk to her or even breathe the same air.

I pulled the keys from my purse and dropped them. I fumbled around trying to find the right key as I picked them up. Someone grabbed me from behind and placed a big hand over my mouth.

I let it happen because I sensed the identity of my assailant. I'd recognize that potent wolf scent anywhere. Marlon.

He shoved me down the stairs. Once we were outside, he removed his hand from my mouth. "Don't scream," he said. "Boss wants to talk."

I glared at him. "Do that again and you're dead."

Across the street, the red Lexus waited.

"I can take it from here, chief," I told Marlon.

Cyrus leaned over and opened the passenger door. I glanced back at the condo windows to make sure Winter hadn't noticed.

I got in and slammed the door. "You've got big balls coming here," I said. "All balls and no sense. That should be your motto."

Cyrus grinned. "That might work with the ladies."

"Yeah, not so much."

"I'm not afraid of your shady boy. He's tough, but I'm not an easy target. A few Kodiak bears learned that the hard way."

I laughed. "This isn't a pissing contest, Cyrus. If Winter wants you dead, you're dead, and there's nothing you or your pack can do about it."

He sat in silence. His pride took a blow.

"Listen," I said. "Everyone knows you're tough. You're the alpha. Maybe don't be your own hype man. Boasting comes off weak."

My words had the opposite effect than I had hoped. "The arrogance of all you power-infused phonies comes off as the weakest," he said. "Strength is something that should be built and earned. Not just gifted."

I guess it is a pissing contest.

"Fine," I said, "let's put some distance between us and Winter."

He drove off, glancing at me sideways. I should have jumped out of the car instead of telling him to drive, but my curiosity got the better of me.

"I just want to talk," he said. "I know I'm not your favorite person, but I think you should hear me out."

Ha. Understatement of the century.

"You have ten minutes," I said. "Don't waste my time."

He quickly grabbed a yellow envelope from the glove compartment.

"Take a look," he said.

I pulled a photo out of the envelope. It was a sick image, depicting a corpse of a man whose face was pale as death itself. His chest had been gashed open, his skull had been bashed in and a nasty bruise circled his neck, a sign of strangulation.

"What is this?" I said, repulsed at the sight.

"One of mine," Cyrus said. "We found him like this along with four more of my shifters. I'd sent them out to meet with the Seattle pack."

"It was an ambush."

"Most definitely. Shapeshifter blood is extremely potent—in specific doses, infusions using our blood can clear up severe infections and, in some cases, reverse the deadly effects of diabetes, cardiac damage, cancer, and even advanced sepsis. It's why we avoid most conditions and survive as long as we do."

"Psycho fucks," I said.

"Yeah, there's a black market for our blood. Rogue shifters run it, mostly exporting it through countries where law enforcement invites payoffs. They market it as a banned miracle drug, being suppressed by the pharmaceutical lobby out of fear too many other products would become obsolete. The wealthy get sick and desperate. They'll pay anything."

I didn't interrupt him. This was the first time he trusted me with real information, not just a line of bullshit.

Cyrus shook his head. "A lot of good people have been tempted to take advantage of this and have suggested we sell some blood to help finance the pack's projects. I've had a string of meetings about this. Darius was present at several of them."

Darius, ugh. I didn't like where this was going.

Cyrus leaned forward, his arms on the wheel. "It's an alpha's job to keep a cool head and call the right shots to protect the pack. Our laws are not just rules to be followed, they also show what the alpha, and therefore his pack, stand for. It is a statement. One of the first laws I passed when I became the Higher Alpha was that the pack would stay clear of the blood market."

"Sounds like the right call," I said.

He shrugged. "If we tried to monitor it, the need would still rise. These basics take terrible care of themselves. Soon, we wouldn't be in control and the billions of them would pay anything to hunters which would quickly drive us to extinction. I instructed my people on this and they listened."

He fell silent. Cyrus usually did a good job of masking his emotions, but his anguish shone through his features. The

Higher Alpha was spooked.

"These dead shifters…" I said.

"Someone drained their bodies dry," he said, hate in his eyes. "Every drop of their blood was gone. All that was left were the empty shells of what had been good men. The murderous scum even scooped out their hearts. The blood is most potent while in the heart chambers."

A chill ran through me. "Cyrus, this is terrible. These black-market hunters have no conscience."

He pushed the photograph back toward me. "His name was Nathan, a generous, loyal man of the pack. A badger shifter. A carpenter. Helped build or design most of the pack's furniture. He left behind a wife and a daughter."

Cyrus had five dead shapeshifters and as their Higher Alpha, he had to not only avenge their deaths, but also shut down the whole blood market that cost them their lives. He had to see it through, or his pack would abandon him for an alpha who would. Cyrus was in a tight spot, but why had he come to me of all people? Surely, he could find closer allies.

"We discovered we had a mole planted in our council," he said. "We made him talk in exchange for a quick death."

I closed my eyes. "Why are you telling me this?"

"Because he told us he was working for Darius."

Ironic how this finally helped him pull his head out of his backside regarding Darius. He had been used by his godfather his entire life.

Cyrus pulled over on a beachside road. It was growing

dark. The sunset painted the sky with fire, its smoldering colors bleeding into the ocean.

"Right in the middle of everything sometimes," I said, "you just have to take a moment to breathe and remember the world isn't only darkness."

We looked at the colors and the hugeness of the sea. Cyrus cracked the windows, and the salty air filled our lungs.

"I do that best when I'm a panther, believe it or not."

"I believe it," I said and closed my eyes to take in more air. "So, the darkest demigod of all, Lord Darius, planted a mole in the pack and thus had instant information about your every move."

Cyrus nodded. "The mole informed Darius of the timetable and the stops the shifter team would make on their way to Seattle."

"Darius has easier ways to make money," I said. "Why this?"

Cyrus looked at me with new eyes. "You're right. I don't think he's going to sell the blood. That's what he wants us to think. It's my belief he intends to use the blood to enhance an army of metamorphic shifters, so they can shift at any time. He won't have to wait."

Metamorphic shifters could morph into anything they wanted, be it real or imaginary, but they needed a meta-morphic moon for that, which didn't happen often, roughly once a century, and only on enchanted lands. If they could shift at any time, anywhere, all reality would be challenged.

There might be dragons breathing fire above our cities, Spinosaurus hordes roaming the freeways, fucking Godzilla popping up at a beach near you.

"Darius wants to build a metamorphic army?" I said. "He wants our worst nightmares to come to life."

"That's only one of the armies he's building. He's on a warpath to best Horror at his own game and get to the finish line first."

Could Darius be behind resurrecting the Savroids and the other wretched creatures hiding behind the gates between realms?

Does he really command so much power?

"Thank you for telling me all of this, but why are you telling me?"

"For the simple reason that I'm hoping you can do something or think of someone or something to help. Also, because I owe you. He's up to something that involves you, Sophie."

I looked at my lap and took a deep breath to suppress frustration. "How many times did I warn you about Darius?"

"What do you want me to say? I got duped," he said. "And it's precisely why I am telling you this now. I want to balance the ledger with you. It might take some time, but I'm making a start."

"Where is Darius now? He must have a base of operations."

Cyrus looked as if I'd just poured hot oil on him. "The

problem with his many bases is they are locked behind charmed gates and portals."

"It's okay," I said. "I know just the supernatural locksmith."

No, no, no... I have to pump my brakes.

Horror and Cyrus on the same team? Winter would never sign off on any of this. Ever. And my savage, deranged relic of a father would hold this over my head for centuries. If Horror took control of the situation, the gutted shifter corpses would be the least of our concerns. Nobody would be able to harness Horror's power if he decided to unleash it.

No, involving Horror would be too dangerous, too lethal. There had to be another way other than handing the keys to Dad.

"Who knows of this?" I said.

"My security team knows. No one else. The panic wouldn't help."

The outline of a man emerged on the sand twenty feet from the car. He wore a brown habit with a hood shielding his head, like a medieval monk. A dark purple aura glowed about him.

Darius pulled down his hood. His eyes gleamed in the twilight.

I could have killed Cyrus. "You set me up."

Cyrus's eyebrows crept up. "I swear I didn't."

"If that's true, then you've been set up again." I said. "And you have a mole infestation in the pack." I opened my door.

"Stay in the car."

I heard his door open. "I'm not staying in the car. This is my mess."

"Cyrus, swallow your pride. I can't guarantee your safety."

He scoffed and walked around the car to join me on the sand.

Darius stepped forward. He opened his arms. "Have I interrupted a romantic moonlight reunion at the beach?"

I scowled at him. "Makeup sex is the best, haven't you heard?"

Darius gave Cyrus the once over. "He doesn't look satisfied."

Gross. I can't believe I started this metaphor.

"We finally have a common goal," I said. "Kicking your ass."

Darius scrutinized Cyrus. "It sickened me to watch you grovel for her attention like a pup in heat," he told his godson. "At least, have the sack to admit you didn't know if you wanted to subdue the witch or serve her."

I yawned. "You really have the wrong witch. I can't be subdued and will never allow anyone to serve me."

Darius glanced to me dismissively. "You talk back like it matters."

"Take off and you won't have to hear it."

Darius raised his hand. A ring of fire spread out like a blaze torrent and brushed against my feet, enclosing me in a fraction of a second. The flames roared and leaped higher like a swirling vortex, growing in intensity and speed, trapping me inside a scorching inferno.

Cyrus leaped back towards the car and vanished.

That's weird.

The world around me cracked and splintered into pieces. I reached for my magic and found a deep, dark void. I mumbled a counter spell to the fire wards, but the words came out fractured, like an unfinished puzzle.

Darius's overpowering magic crashed into me. I winced and shuddered from both the shock from the invasive force and the pain from the scalding heat.

There was an odd calm on his face, evil and unsettling, yes, but also content. My torture gave him peace.

"This is a custom spell built specifically for you," he said as he circled me. "My insurance policy if you will."

"You're that afraid of me?"

So, my mouth still works.

Darius paused to think. "I studied your magic while you were staying at the Umbra and then the pack compound, your preferences and aversions when it came to employing it, looking for your Achilles' heel."

"It won't work," I said.

"It already has. There is no counter spell for this fire ward. I enhanced it with my own blood. As long as I breathe, it will keep burning and blocking your powers."

A tiny bit of magic dripped into my core. "There's an easy fix to that."

"Indeed," he agreed. "All you have to do is ask me to release you and we can start all over."

The bastard was using magic out in the open, all rules of magic and consequences be damned. He had gone completely rogue.

"Tell me, Luna," he said. "Are you sharing your mentor's bed yet?"

That came out of left field. Of what interest...

"The reason I ask is because if you have mated, then you would have seen Winter in an unrestrained environment, and you would know something you otherwise would have only suspected. There's more to him than he lets on."

I kept chanting lunar spells, urging my body to replenish. "Your sick games won't work, Darius."

"You don't know what he is, do you? An Immortal who recovers from complete shut-down in a matter of weeks is more than an anomaly. Consider this a friendly warning. Don't sleep next to him with both your eyes closed."

The trickle of magic increased, tickling my fingertips.

Keep talking, you megalomaniac.

"If you have something to say, just say it, Darius."

He stepped closer to the fire ring. Another inch and I might have enough energy to strike.

"Come on, Luna Mae, you can't be this daft, you know it, you feel it, you can almost hear what I'm trying to say."

"I really can't," I said.

Darius raised his hand above his head. "I'm going to cool

down the wards, just enough so we can talk."

The flames pulled back a touch, shorter and weakened. A soft breeze blew through the fire onto my face. Magic poured into me like a spring rain.

I didn't know if the magic had come from me, the moon or even Horror. I didn't care. It was mine now to command.

Sizzling energy poured out of me and cut through the fire ward, blasting Darius backwards. A time portal opened up and sucked him in, imploding into a rainbow of colors.

Take that, boorish demigod.

For all his stalking and grandstanding, Darius had no idea I had extra energy reserves or that I could control time portals.

Shout out to Dad.

The fire wards suddenly surged anew, rising higher around me like a prison chamber in hell.

I pushed my hand through the flames. My skin melted instantly. I cried out.

What the fuck was I thinking? Of course, my skin would melt.

With Darius gone, the ward burned out of control. I closed my eyes and prepared for burning alive as I walked through the fire.

All those dreams of me burning over and over were finally coming to fruition, my worst fears realized.

"Sophie!" It was Cyrus's voice. I wasn't sure if it was real or false hope.

Cyrus walked up to me, a growing blur coming into focus. The smugness had drained from his eyes. In his sparkling irises, a new determination flickered. "I'll get you out of there."

I shook my head and yelled, "These aren't normal flames. Even your panther form would get barbecued on the spot."

Keeping his eyes on me, Cyrus shivered, his lips drawing back in a grotesque grin. His body lengthened, his eyes turned into two large pools of black, as he morphed into something feathery.

A gigantic golden eagle stared at me, spreading its massive wings.

Even in such agony, I was aghast. "You're a metamorphic shifter. Does Darius know?"

"You want to burn to ash or get out of here?"

Point taken.

I'd heard that metamorphic shifters could grunt and form monosyllabic words while shifted, but Cyrus was next level.

What do you know? I wasn't the only one holding back.

Two clawed feet scooped me up by my shoulders. The eagle's wings flapped, the flames singeing their edges, and lifted us away. In one deep breath, we were soaring over the sand and then the darkening ocean.

My head spun. My heart thundered in my ears. Cyrus swooped higher, as if heading for the canopy of stars above.

Chapter 19

THE SOFT OCEAN BREEZE filled my lungs. Waves rolled onto La Jolla Beach under a half-moon that cast its light like silver glitter on the water. My magic loved quiet nights like this when my elemental core could drink in copious amounts of aquatic and lunar energy, but tonight I jogged with a panic in my heart that wouldn't be calmed.

Time was of the essence. Chaos had left as soon as I explained I had blasted Darius into a time portal. I didn't quite have the power yet to control teleporting with accuracy, but Chaos felt certain Darius was not far away and would soon find his way back to his own portals. Chaos promised he'd locate him before Darius locked himself inside his own domain, and thus making it impossible for any of us to reach him.

My body felt worn down. I'd been running for a while, sensing shadows behind me and on all sides, following me at a distance. Chaos had enlisted a few of his black demon hounds to watch over me.

In my mind I killed Darius for the thirtieth time. I fantasized about sliding my enchanted sword through his ribcage while drawing his life force out of his eye sockets. It was the next best thing to actually getting my hands on him. He would not stop until he found a way to abduct me, I was certain of that. We had to strike now and hope to catch him off guard.

It wouldn't be easy. Darius always planned ahead. He didn't leave anything to chance. If he had placed moles on the pack council, it was a certainty he had other intelligence sources, maybe within Immortal Councils or even the Deep Down. We couldn't alert anyone, or Darius might discover our plans and work on setting another trap.

A demon hound howled behind me. I picked up speed, wanting to disappear into the night and melt with the elements.

Winter was off to the Umbra domain to update the Shadow Master and ask for the Order's assistance. He couldn't help himself. He might have left the Seventh, but his need to respect and defer to authority still burned inside him.

The demon hounds got closer, sniffing out the air so loud I could hear how they flared the nostrils on their drooling snouts.

I glanced over my shoulder. In the distance, I saw a tall, human-shaped figure pop into existence out of nowhere. I spun back and sprinted toward the figure, willing my legs to go as fast as they could.

Chaos brushed his long hair back with his fingers. The moonlight drifted over his hardened features. Five huge demon hounds rushed to meet him, tongues lapping at his legs.

I looked up at him, short of breath. "Tell me you have good news."

A demon hound bit his hand. Chaos cursed and slapped the death doggie aside. "I found Darius," he said. "The third-eye vision had to be employed, so in all probability, Horror saw through it too."

"Okay, so is this a good-news bad-news kind of thing?"

He made a face. "Mm, more like a bad-news, good-news, bad-news, bad-news, bad-news—"

"Okay, I get it. Horror knowing we're looking for Darius is not good."

When Chaos spoke, his voice was measured and commanding. "To escape the time portal, Darius had to anchor his power to his strongest source of energy. The Palace of Alcaraz."

"Is that present tense Palace of Alcaraz? I remember from an *Ancient Civilizations* class it was wiped from existence thousands of years ago."

"The palace is gone, but Darius kept a bridge portal open under the ruins. The magic there is so robust he uses it both to replenish his energy and to shield his presence."

"Well, that sucks."

Chaos frowned. "The worst part—"

"Wait, Darius being undetectable at his stronghold is not the worst part?"

"If you listen…" he said. "The problem I speak of is a logistical problem. We have to cross a bridge through a void. This bridge is extremely flimsy. Only one can cross at a time, or it will collapse into the infernal abyss below. And it's a true void down there. No magic is possible if you fall. None."

Ugh. "That *is* worse."

"But…" Chaos said, scrunching his face, "if, say, a crazy person managed to cross the bridge and penetrate the portal, said fool might, in theory, then open the back gates to allow a fucking army to march through. Assuming Darius hasn't pureed their flesh into a bloody mush by then."

I patted his shoulder. "That's it then. We're leaving now before he retreats deeper into his domain."

"What? Without Jonas Frost and his All-Shadow Band?"

"We're the only ones who can teleport. I'll send Carter to Umbra to fill in Winter and the Shadow Master. I'll cross the bridge and open the gates for them when they arrive."

I thought his head would explode. "Luna! I say something senseless, and you immediately jump face first into the danger. It doesn't have to be you who risks everything to open the gates."

"You did say a crazy person was needed for this."

"And your first thought was… *Hey, that's me?*"

"Chaos," I said, my voice stern, "we're wasting time we don't have."

"Alas, I suppose I'm to go as well," he said, bothered. "And coax a few death puppies along as security escort."

"That would be good. Thanks, bro."

Chaos sighed. "Can we pop around the shops before we go? I want to buy one of those t-shirts that says, *I'm with stupid*."

I laughed. "This was your idea, genius."

"Right," he said. "So, you wear the shirt."

THE AIR IN THE underground tunnels beneath the land once occupied by the Persian Palace of Alcaraz was asphyxiating. My lungs swelled to inhale the trace amounts of oxygen swimming in a sea of unbreathable gases and ash.

Chaos shot past me, chasing after a frenzied demon hound.

I stretched my neck to follow their manic chase. The demon hound jumped over a huge, exposed root, stopped, sniffed the ground and barked his head off.

"Get him to stop," I told Chaos. "We're supposed to be sneaking in."

The hound licked the root, lifted his head and howled. Chaos's boot connected with its behind. The beast was lifted off his feet and flew into a pile of rock, whimpering.

"They're sensing something," Chaos said.

Yeah, hell fires and sulfur fumes probably.

We kept moving ahead, past strange shrubs the color of charcoal and oddly carved stones. Breathing became harder as the air grew hotter.

My mind struggled to acknowledge the hard facts. Darius had come after me too many times already. He had abducted Winter and Arsha. Next, he might go after those closest to me who weren't immortal to force my cooperation. He wouldn't hesitate to kill someone I loved to prove he was serious. I had to deal with him, now, no matter the cost, or more of my people would suffer by his hand.

I bent down and yanked a handful of purplish grass out of the ground. My palm lit up, incinerating the grass.

Chaos stepped next to me. "What the hell? Are you trying to warn Darius there are intruders approaching?"

I shrugged. "You said your cloaking is foolproof."

He grabbed my chin. "I say a lot of things, tiresome tot. We're too close to be pushing our luck. Look!"

Ahead, I saw a narrow hanging bridge maybe fifty feet from us. It was the shabbiest bridge imaginable, hacked together with clumps of coiled wire, misshapen wooden planks and cardboard, all held together with rope.

"Flimsy?" I said accusingly to Chaos. "You were being generous."

I made it to the abyss edge where the bridge began. I should not have looked down. A gaping mouth of jutted rocks and sharp branches stretched down to infinity. Glimmering dots sparked from too far down to know what flying predators were there, waiting to chomp on you as you fell forever.

On the far end of the bridge, a portal swirled like a steam tornado, blue flames slinking along its base.

It had to be fire.

I glanced back at Chaos. "You sure we can't teleport to the other side?"

He scoffed. "For the tenth time, no. Our teleporting powers don't work here. And you can't teleport into a stream of perpetual power. Unless you want to be split into a trillion energy molecules."

"Okay... stop repeating yourself."

Chaos stood silent for a moment. "You got this, little sis. If I had to pick any lunatic for this in the whole mad world, it would be you."

"Gee, thanks."

His hand landed gently on mine. "Don't let Darius fuck with your head. Don't let him get to you. Go in, open the gates, get out."

"Oh, that's all? I guess I'm all set then."

"I thought it sounded good. Did I say I'm rooting for you?"

Only one way to end his motivational speeches...

I stepped on the bridge—barely wider than my hips. It covered an expanse of at least 30 feet. Every fiber in me told me I would fall straight through and into the abyss when my second foot moved onto the bridge.

I started to shake and took the step. The bridge swung a little and creaked, but I was on the bridge, all of me, and I had not fallen through.

I gripped the ropes and took a step and then another. The bridge swung more. I stopped. My arms shook intensely. I took four more steps.

"Sister?" Chaos called out.

"I feel the portal's power," I said. "It's ancient and... awesome."

"Just get closer," Chaos suggested, anxiously.

He was already doubting the sanity of the plan, I could feel it. If Carter didn't reach Umbra in time, I'd find myself knee deep in some real shit.

I took one more step. The portal whirled faster, spreading its magic like tentacles, inviting me closer. If I attempted to access it without a strong shield, it'd chew me down whole and throw my bones out.

The bridge suddenly shook violently. A creature big as a humpback whale stretched a huge, clawed hand from below to grab at me. Its body was long and slick with spikes sticking out along its back. Its face was shapeless save for a round hole in the middle that probably served as mouth or nose or both. I could feel something else spinning above my head. I didn't want to look up and risk losing my nerve.

"Abort, get off the bridge!" Chaos yelled.

The portal spun out of control. Inhaling deep, I ducked under the second swipe of the huge creature's claw and broke into a sprint across the bridge.

No portal was going to be my end. I was the daughter of the Master of Eternal and Perpetual Creatures. Darius would hit me with fire again, more intense than before. I knew it. But I was a mist rider.

Bring it, demigod!

The portal hauled me in with a strong gravitational force. I fought it at first and then I let go. I let my magic meld with the spinning energy of the portal as if we were one.

The blue flames leaped higher, expanding to encase the portal.

Too late to turn back.

I glided right through the ring of fire. The flames licked at my feet and hands. I felt nothing.

The portal snapped shut behind me. I was inside Darius's dark domain. Trapped. The only way was forward. Just me and the Persian King of Kings.

A rock crystal pathway welcomed me; the walls shimmered with a silver iridescence like mirrors. Energy and magic streams were plentiful here. A man stood at the far end, a translucent golden cloud hovering above him.

The man had dark eyes and short, brown hair. His skin glowed golden, his lips a crimson red. His gilded silky robe hung loosely on him. A finely forged leaf crown rested on his head. He cut an imposing, regal figure far beyond all the nobilities of the basic world.

Darius had celestial eyes that looked right through me.

His power smoldered about him, spreading everywhere. I shuddered. Defeating him in his realm seemed an impossibility.

"You are a curiosity," he said, his voice both quiet and booming. "You have traveled to a place that none has ever traveled."

A desire to kneel before him swelled inside. I resisted the urge, driving my nails inside my palms to awaken my own magic.

"You cannot continue on the path you have chosen, Lord Darius," I said, gulping down my fear. "I refuse to be your pawn."

A metallic purple haze emanated from him as he lost patience. "We two together could have accomplished anything. Even now, there is still time to reach for the stars."

There was not just menace in his voice, but something wistful.

"Understand me," he went on. "I am not driven by greed nor lust nor any petty emotion. I have ruled and I have been feared. Under my hand, empires rose to greatness. My subjects thrived. I brought stability and prosperity. I built roads to connect continents. I stood up for the world of magic and the mythic gods. Darius the Undestroyable is one of the key authors of the history of the world. Your basics would still be in the dark ages had I turned away."

"There is truth to what you're saying, but the fact you think you're acting noble in this time is what concerns me, Darius. You believe yourself to be leading a crusade, but like the crusaders you've mistaken your own vision of the world as permission to violently repress all other views."

Okay, I wrote that in a college essay, but it still works.

Darius's face hardened. "There is no way out."

I strained my neck to peek beyond him. "Really? Isn't that a big gate just back there?"

"I tried to be reasonable," he said. "You came here, you violated our sanctity and now we must subdue you the hard way."

"Dude," I said. "*We*? Really? This isn't ancient Persia. Your subjects are all dead. Long ago. The world doesn't need another great and mighty king."

I blasted him with a force field. Darius stepped forward and flung it aside easily, but my goal was accomplished. Behind him, I saw the fabled gate intricately carved out of the silver wall in the shape of a tear.

Bingo Bango Bingo.

He followed my gaze. The brown of his eyes turned to black coal. His power spread like furious tentacles, swarming my energy core.

The first wave of fire cracked through the crystal floor, encircling me. Another wave roared down from above, collapsing the dome of my shield.

My etheric essence was burning up. The heat penetrated

skin and muscle to lick at my core like a predator starved for magic. A headache exploded in my skull like a sledgehammer through stone. He was cooking me alive.

No, I am descended from the morning mists.

A drip of magic turned into a gusher pouring out of me like a cascade, cooling me. Fluid energy burst from my chest and stormed down on the crackling flames like a tempest, swamping the room.

The fire failed under the torrential water assault and fizzled out.

Fury strained the eyes of the Lord and High Ruler of this empty place.

From inside his silk robe, he drew out a sword.

Magic from above fluttered to the floor like liquid mercury. I raised my hands to reabsorb the silver magic into my core.

Darius's eyes widened. The sword slid out of his grip and clanged to the floor before my feet, shattering into pieces.

I should have been stunned by my own power, but I had no time for perspective. Darius was reduced, his energy expended only to be quickly gathered up and trapped in my core.

Now I built a cyclone and thrust it forward with both hands. Darius fought back with his own force field. Our energies collided, hissing, in a colossal battle of wills.

With a final effort, I poured ley line energy into my cyclone. Darius lost footing. The Persian King of Kings lost concentration and my cyclone quickly gobbled him up, trapping him inside an energy sphere.

Someone began clapping behind me.

The fuck?

I spun. Horror stood, tall and powerful, dressed in fitting black armor and a crimson cape over his wide shoulders. A bronze axe shone in his right hand.

"Bravo, Daughter," Horror said. "My involvement was minor. You did most of the heavy lifting. Let's just say I nudged your bike a little."

I stared at him, dumbfounded.

Darius growled from within the sphere. He slammed against the energy field again and again, only to be zapped back.

Horror laughed. "He's learning he never stood a chance."

From Scylla to Charybdis...

"You know the Greek saying," he said. "I'm impressed. Another man's daughter might have thought *between a rock and a hard place*, but not my brilliant student of Anthropology and Ethnology."

"Stop reading my thoughts," I said. "How are you even in here? Never mind, I'd rather not know that answer."

Horror took a step forward. "All your life, you've wondered about your aversion to fire. It began when you were a newborn and I bathed you in the eternal fires of youth to bestow you eternal life."

I said nothing.

"Those eternal fires also gave you an ability you have not tapped. If you only believe it, then fire can no longer touch you, my beautiful flower of the dawn, it cannot hurt you. For you are fire."

Horror's magic pulled me to him—my feet dragged along the floor like I was a doll made of straw. I didn't resist. I was too exhausted.

His hands leaped to my shoulders. He touched his forehead to mine. "I'll help you. With this breath, I gift you the power of fire."

He pulled back and breathed out onto my forehead. Adrenaline rushed through my veins. My heartbeat thundered in my chest. My father's magic sunk into all my cells like a supernatural IV.

All my anger, all my anxiety vanished. Elation permeated every cell in my body and every thought in my mind.

"What did you do?" I whispered. "Is it drugs?"

"I erased confusion in your essence. Now you know who you are."

My father's hand came alive with a ball of fire. He sprinkled the flames on the floor like confetti. "Touch the fire, Luna."

I hesitated. I slid my palm over the blaze. The fire recognized my father's blood in me. When I ran my fingers through it, the red flames barely touched them, meeting my skin softly like a timid kiss.

Horror smiled. "My masterwork."

Those words brought me to my senses. "If you think I am yours to rule after coming all this way to make sure Darius would pose no threat to our world, you will be sorely disappointed."

A wicked grin crept onto Horror's face. He glanced at Darius. "Let's end him now, Daughter. I'll show you how. A final lesson."

I shook my head. "You should leave. The Shadow Warriors will be here any minute. They will decide what needs to be done with him."

"You would trust a cult over your father?"

"I would trust a snake over you."

"Very well," Horror said. "I will give you space to process. Fatherhood's tough. Much harder than war. Take some time off, flower. You've earned it."

I blinked and Horror was gone. His magic lingered, waiting, floating, watching my every move.

The silver gate!

I ran through the sad palace to the gate and found a small, gold skeleton key hanging from a metal peg on the wall. I felt around the gate for a lock for the longest time, unable to locate it.

Sweat covered my brow. My fingers trembled. Teleporting out of this breeding cocoon of magic was out of the question. My molecules would come apart at the seams.

A click. Finally, I slid the key inside the keyhole and turned it. The gate unglued itself from the wall and creaked open slowly. *Home Depot would definitely have a spray to help with that. Gram would know.*

I stepped out into a kaleidoscope dreamscape. Winter was already running when I spotted him crossing the wide, sturdy bridge. He had his shining sword in his right hand and a league of armored Shadow Warriors marching in formation behind him.

The Shadow Warriors stormed into the portal.

Winter lingered at the gate with me. "You alright?"

Loaded question. "You're here, so yeah."

"Where else would I be? You're always the destination."

Would it be wrong to jump him right here?

Two Shadow Warriors marched out dragging Darius between them. His hands were cuffed with a magnetic field clamp. He lifted his eyes to shoot me an odious glance. His face became an ugly contortion of rage.

We watched the Shadow Warriors hurry him across the bridge.

As a recent student of history, it was breathtaking to realize that this was how the legendary Darius, the ancient Persian King of Kings, came to his end. He was marched quietly across a bridge in a kaleidoscope dreamland having fallen by my hand.

How the mighty have fallen.

Chapter 20

I woke at the first touch of dawn. I searched for Winter in the dark and didn't find him. My whole body was tense and aching still, as my system tried to burn off Darius's dark magic from my energy core.

It might have been worse. Darius could have won the fight if he had absorbed my magic instead. Who knows what would have happened if Horror hadn't followed me there to give me that little extra oomph.

I got out of bed and walked down the hallway. The shower was running in the bathroom. I wasn't the only one who had a hard time staying asleep.

We were polar opposites, Winter and I. He was ice and I was fire. Or so I had been told. His cool demeanor and my fiery demeanor were always sources of attraction, I now realized.

The shower stopped running right as I was about to give

in to temptation and join Winter. He needed and deserved the privacy, even if for just a few minutes, under the hot showerhead. He'd had an incredibly challenging day. We both needed a break, especially since I could not wait much longer to tell him the enormous revelations I'd been holding back.

Winter came out of the bathroom with a white towel around his waist. His upper body looked even more powerful and defined when wet. *Wow*. I wanted to poke those muscles with my finger until it hurt.

Focus, Luna.

"You should let your restorative powers heal those tattoo wounds" I said, pointing at the still damaged skin across his chest.

Winter walked to the window and cracked open the blinds. Stripes of light spilled into the room. His biceps tensed as he leaned against the wall.

"Maybe tomorrow," he said, knowing I wanted to talk.

We walked back to the bedroom. I lay on the bed and watched him dress, completely enthralled in the ritual. Winter extended one arm to get it through the sleeve of his navy-blue button up shirt. His pecs and abs moved like they were separate life forms.

He winked at me as he buttoned the shirt, his fingers moving skillfully as if they existed for no other reason. I breathed in all the joy of being in this room with this man that took my breath away.

"What's next?" I asked.

He sat next to me on the bed. I nestled myself inside his arms.

"Today, I don't care. All is well for now, and I want us to live in the moment for a bit," he said. "The future can fuck off."

Wouldn't that be nice?

I sucked in a sharp breath. "There was a moment with Darius that I feared not making it out alive."

His muscles locked tighter around me. "When Carter found me and told me what you had planned," he said, "I swore if you didn't die, I'd spank your butt like a child."

Say what now?

"What were you thinking, Luna? Going after Darius by yourself, traveling through his portals?"

I pushed up out of his arms and sat up. "I was thinking Darius needed to be stopped before he hurt anyone else."

"You should have waited for me and stuck to the plan."

"He was depleted," I said, sharply. "The last thing I would allow was that psychotic to have ample time to replenish his energy and gather his armies."

"I understand, but the answer can't always be you risking your life."

"Everyone was at risk, not just me," I reminded him.

He buried his head in his hands. "You're not everyone, Luna," he said and then sat up to face me. "You're one of one. We all need you to survive."

"I'm your one, but that doesn't mean I'm better than anyone."

"Listen, I have experience you lack. My magic, my power, they are more disciplined than yours. I don't fear pain and I'm not driven by emotion. You are untrained, impulsive and not synced with your true essence."

Wow. Quite a smackdown.

"Am I supposed to clap or something? Even with my untrained, impulsive nature, I was the one who captured Darius and opened the gate to give your shadow buddies access to his entire energy domain."

Winter threw me a savage glance that could have shaken a statue. His eyes had the ferocity of a lone predator.

"About that," he said, coolly. "Exactly how did you trap Darius inside his own domain, right beneath his strongest source of energy, the Palace of Alcaraz? You'd need a similar power boost to have any chance."

Uh-oh.

"The silver portal contains some of the most concentrated magic on the planet," he went on. "When you entered it, a series of defense mechanisms were activated. Darius's power fed off those mechanisms, amplifying him to the potency of a nuclear detonation."

I turned away, unable to hold his gaze any longer. Why was he being so damn irritating? He said we should relax!

"There's more," he said, apparently on a roll. "When the Shadow convoy arrived at Umbra, they noticed that Darius was depleted of magic energy, his core drained, his essence weakened.”

“Really? Huh.”

Winter frowned. “You still have a ton of his magic.”

Other people tended to walk away from landmines, I seemed to step right on them. “Maybe what you’re sensing is my colossal frustration.”

He shook his head. “It aches, right? Carrying all that hostile energy.”

I stared at him. “Well, aren’t you the Farmers’ Almanac for magical climates. Is there anything you can’t predict?”

“I’m not hearing a denial in there.”

I bit my lip. Why was I fighting him? I had already made up my mind I’d come clean about Horror, but I guess Winter was uniquely gifted at triggering my most immature responses.

“I think you might need a drink,” I said.

He arched an eyebrow. “I know that look. What storm is brewing?”

I lay back on the pillows, making room for him next to me. He sat on the edge of the bed, troubled.

You wanted answers... careful what you wish for.

Even choosing a way to begin was difficult.

“Remember when I told you Horror knew I was a mist rider?”

His face shut down at the sound of Horror’s name.

“That’s not all he knows,” I said, my voice trailing off.

He waited a moment to speak. It was excruciating.

"He knows about Penelope's prophecy, then? He knows you will be the one to kill him?"

Right. He wasn't going to make it easy.

"I'm sure he knows that, too, but that's not the thing."

"It's not?" he said. "So, there's a more dangerous thing?"

I had to fucking just come out and say it. Winter hated Horror enough to want to wipe his entire bloodline off the Earth. He had a right to know that bloodline had been sleeping in his arms.

My eyes flew up to him. "What he knows is, ah, that I'm his long-lost daughter. The daughter he planned to turn into an ultimate weapon."

A quick twinge of pain flexed in his blue eyes. Winter said nothing.

I inhaled. "Everywhere I turn, Horror is there. He talks to me both in the flesh and telepathically. When I fought the Earth troll, he gave me a hand by erasing all memories of it in the basic world. He's offered to teach me, make me stronger, help me become a true mist rider. He keeps dropping skills at my feet, like teleporting, the way Chaos does with the blue smoke."

His face stiffened. He was probably doing the math and realizing Chaos was another of Horror's progeny.

All I wanted was for him to say something, anything, even yell. Anything would be better than trying to guess what was in his mind.

"And Darius..." I went on. "I don't know exactly how, but Horror somehow boosted me so I would defeat Darius and absorb the energy he used to attack me into my own core."

That last one must have done it, I was certain of that. Being Horror's daughter was one thing. Actively having him guide me was another.

He lifted a brow. "And when you crossed into the silver domain, did you know Horror would be there to help?"

"No, I had no idea he could just teleport there. Chaos said it would be impossible to teleport inside a stream of constant power."

Winter gritted his teeth. Maybe I should stop mentioning Chaos.

"And there you have it. You've been protecting Horror's daughter this whole time. The last thing you wanted. I am sure."

He reached out, took my hand and pulled me closer.

"You finally told me."

Finally told me?

"You knew?"

"How would I not know?" he said. "Have you met me?"

"For how long?"

He took my face in both hands, exploring my eyes. "When you've been around as long as I have, you know. You feel things. Situations arise and there's a hidden math only the very experienced understand."

"Okay," I said, "but you're not a seer."

"No, but it was plain to see that even though your essence is that of a mist rider, there's more there, something equally old and powerful. And then there was Chaos. For someone who never shuts up about anything, he never talked about the father you two share. That has always bothered me. When you told me you had met Horror in battle and you were left standing, that was as good as a final confirmation."

It made sense and yet... "Why didn't you say something?"

"It was your truth, Luna. A revelation like that takes time to process. Life is hard for basics and Immortals alike. I wish I had been there to support you."

"But you weren't, because of Horror. He already tried to kill you once, because of your connection to me. It won't be the last time."

"If he wants me dead, I'll be dead."

"Please don't say it like that, Jonas. We're going to find a way. If it comes to that, you should run for the hills and lie low."

"You mean, run away from you?"

I nodded. "Being with me comes with grave risks. I wouldn't blame you. Horror is more interested in keeping me alive than killing me, but you and everyone in my life are fair game."

"Luna, if I wanted a safe life, I'd have become a monk."

"And what do you want? Danger?"

"You. Us. Anything other than living by a murderous despot's whims and fancy. The fact that I've fallen for you hasn't changed a thing. I'd be fighting by your side anyway."

His chest stiffened at my touch. "I'm just glad you're not mad."

"Who said I'm not?" he said, raising an eyebrow.

He got up, yanking me up by the hand so I fell against him. Winter pushed me back until I was sandwiched between the wall and his solid body. His lips crushed on mine, pressing, biting, submitting me to his will. My heart was an organ of lust now, going from emotion to emotion without holding back.

"I don't care about your father, or your mother, or the stars in the sky, or whatever magic brought you into this world. You make everything matter again," he said, breathing heavily in my ear. "I can let go of the past and crave a future. Not only are you good, but you taste good."

A sudden fear grabbed me. "Darius warned me about you."

He chuckled. "Of course, he did." He kissed me again and again.

"He said you're not a regular Immortal."

"I'm not."

"He said you're dangerous."

"What do you want me to say? That I'm not?"

I met his gaze. "He also said that to become a Shadow Warrior, you had to kill someone you loved."

Winter pulled back, a dark glow in his eyes. "Sounds like him."

"That's not an answer. I need to know." I closed my eyes. "I thought I didn't, but I do. I know I'm being selfish."

Silence hung in the air.

Winter let go, his arms falling to his sides. "Did I kill someone I loved? What do you honestly think, Luna Mae?"

Were his words revealing? I couldn't tell. "I don't think anything, that's why I'm asking."

He sat on the bed. "As centuries slide away, Immortals tend to reinvent themselves. I'm not the same person I was a thousand years ago. I evolve over time like every other being. There is no point reconnecting to what I once was any more than you reconnecting to your infancy." He sighed. "I have regrets, thousands of them, but killing someone close to me, someone who trusted me, is not one of them."

My eyes filled with tears. "Thank you for that," I said. "I should have never let Darius mess with my head. Jonas, my mother has significant pull over Chaos. She convinced him to steal me from my crib to protect me from Horror. Horror was hurt by that betrayal and chose to blame it all on Chaos. He will figure out your part in this if he hasn't already. He's incredibly vindictive."

"Who's your source?"

"Horror himself. He and I have had various, um, chats."

Winter remained stoic. "He's more fucked up than your brother."

"Tell me about it. I mean, they're both infinitely fucked up."

He walked to the window and drew the blinds wide open. Sun spilled into the room like a cleansing agent.

I hurried to wrap my arms around him from behind, face against his back. His body tensed, then he spun around to take me in his arms.

"God, I missed you," he said, kissing my lips softly.

I felt lightheaded. I reached for the buttons on his dress shirt. He grabbed both my hands, stopping me from going any further.

"Let me just look at you," I said. My breath caught in my throat. "All of you. Please."

I started unbuttoning the front of his shirt. This time he let me. I went slowly—each button felt like discovery. I opened his shirt, resting my hands on his warm, naked chest. His temperature reached every part of me. I pushed the shirt back over his hulking shoulders and softy kissed his clavicle.

He reacted to my lips with a soft moan as if all toxic energy melted out of his body. I pulled the shirt down his arms until it fell off him.

Winter wrapped those powerful arms around me and lifted my lips to his. The promises his tongue made to mine with its sweet swirling desire, reassured my entire being that that man was mine.

I pulled back enough to see him. "We don't have to hold back. Everyone knows we're together."

He reached under my t-shirt to unclasp my bra. "You don't understand the magnitude of the reverberations we'd produce," he whispered.

"I don't. I also don't care."

His hands roamed my body, hungry and commanding. I began panting and wrapped a leg around his thigh.

He took hold of my leg and set it back down. "I'm only a man in the end. Don't do this to me," he said and nibbled on my lower lip. "It's not safe yet."

"When will it be…" I began to say.

Magic rolled across the room like a warm river of air as Winter's wards warned us of a visitor. Someone knocked on the door.

Winter pulled his shirt back on and ran out of the bedroom. When he came back, Kirsi was with him.

"You have news?" I said.

"You two are like teenagers," she said. "I swear."

"Kirsi…" I said. "Why are you here?"

"Düsternis came back. He's mega pissed at what's going on. Hordes of supernatural creatures have amassed at the Muir Woods portals. Thousands of them. They've captured twelve hedge witches who live in the woods. An army of metamorphic shifters is on the move from the east to join them."

My god. I'm never getting laid.

Chapter 21

FOG HUNG LOW IN the giant redwood trees, shrouding the dark woods in a mystical aura. The forest bed glistened like a wet blanket. Walking through Muir Woods was like descending into an alien world, away from civilization, even before entering the enchanted part of the forest.

The Valkyries and the Shadow Warriors moved like phantoms, guided by their sharp senses, deciphering shapes and sounds as they floated through the primordial pathways of the fabled woods.

My hands glowed producing a steady stream of light for our advancing party. It was a humbling feeling to be so small among the tallest living things, the coastal redwoods, waiting for an assault of demons and monsters.

Some of those trees were over 1,000 years old yet were born long after the man walking next to me.

Winter didn't want to enlist any other Immortals for this

mission. I understood, but if it were up to me, I'd have taken any fighters available. As it were, we had ten Valkyries and twenty-two Shadow Warriors, but each one of them was worth at least three regular Immortals.

We came to the translucent energy wall that was the gateway to the enchanted woods, visible only to supernaturals and magic users. We squeezed ourselves through the wall one-by-one to the other side.

The climate inverted. The pleasantly cool early September evening grew deadly cold. Snowflakes as big as my hand crumbled on the branches and sank into the wet soil.

The trail we walked was frozen with thin cracking ice. A frosty blast swirled, chilling my bones. The sound of sleigh bells rang out in the distance.

I clutched Winter's hand. His gaze did not leave the white path ahead.

"It's the magic of the forest," he said. "It plays tricks on intruders."

The wind chimed and bellowed. An eerie voice echoed through the trees. "*Who walks the winter woods at night?*"

My legs couldn't move fast enough. I'd rather fight twenty demons than face a single forest specter.

The path took us straight to a snow-covered, gargantuan tree, taller and thicker than any in Muir Woods. Our way was blocked. Clusters of sharp icicles broke from the tree branches and shot out at us like rapid fire.

"Take cover!" Winter yelled.

I dived behind a tree. Winter rolled over me.

Someone screeched. An icicle had punctured a Valkyrie's thigh. The Immortal Sisterhood gathered around their injured warrior.

"The icicles are poisoned with bonshek," Kirsi said. "The icicle was removed, but some shards are still inside Hildra's leg."

Bonshek slowed immortal cell regeneration down to a drip. If the icicle had pierced the Valkyrie's heart, she would already be among the dead.

"Assign an escort to take Hildra back," Winter said.

This wasn't good. The battle hadn't even started, and we were already down two fighters.

A bone-chilling shriek broke through the quiet. A flock of flying creatures dived toward us. They plunged from a portal hovering among the trees and punched easily through thick frozen branches.

The warriors around me raised their blades. The creatures swooped down just missing the tips of the swords and flew back up to circle above us.

I knew not what creatures they were. Their black fur, leathery wings, short snouts and pointy ears suggested some hellish crossbreed of large bats and small bears.

An ear-splitting thunder tore the gigantic tree in half, snow and ice crashing down with the exploding timber. A horde of metamorphic shifters slipped through the two fallen half sections of the massive trunk, their human forms still intact. They inched their way forward in silence, a motley crew of half-naked, vicious looking titans, hungering to shift.

Shadow Warriors and Valkyries closed ranks in close order formation, swords in hand, under multiple layers of force shields. Winter and I joined them in the middle. Going through us would be a tall order for any army.

The morphs stopped and quickly stripped down to nothing. Their skin thickened and blistered, fur spurting and sheathing their exploding bodies. Last time, I'd been able to halt their shifting by commanding the metamorphic moon. This time, there was nothing to command. The morphs shifted without the aid of the rare, enchanted moon phase.

Darius had succeeded wildly in his quest to build an army of monsters.

The newly shifted beasts bellowed as one, huge jaws snapping and biting at the cold air. Some among them had shifted into recognizable, although supersized forms: wolves, tigers, lions, bears and hyenas. The rest could be anything, from mixing two different breeds, to near impossibilities like giant mosquitos, to literal, unimaginable monster concoctions.

A massive winged Savroid snarled as he towered above the metamorphic mob, a twelve-foot-tall beast that sent chills through my lungs.

"Ravage flesh!" he yelled. "Grind bones!"

Behind him, the metamorphic horde broke into a chant, their snarls mixing into a soul scraping cacophony.

"Ravage, ravage, grind, grind!"

Another horde of supernatural creatures burst through the trees, surrounding us—scent phantoms. These specters of the night came in all sizes and shades, they looked like skeletal x-rays and could slide their bony fingers into you, snatching your essence. They could shimmy through force fields if they attacked as one in great numbers. Swords couldn't touch the phantoms, no material weapons could. Only scent spells could deter them, and I'd never studied those hard enough, assuming I would never need them.

The bat bears descended from the sky, unfurling their wings like parachutes, huge talons poised to jab into flesh.

The big Savroid barked, brandishing a double-headed sledgehammer.

We plodded forward, slowly, pushing back the first line of morphs. The scent phantoms swept over us as one, scratching and scraping to tear through our force shield.

Winter and the Shadow Warriors jumped out of the shield to take the attack to the morphs. I reinforced the shield around myself and the Valkyries and zapped the scent phantoms with energy to keep them focused on us and away from the Shadow Warriors.

The ground shook now with the hammering of heavy boots marching. Düsternis and a convoy of twelve Magistrates, Chazona among them, came into view. They wore silver chain mail and helmets, their faces alarmingly grim.

Winter broke from the fight, the blade of his sword painted crimson. "Hold!" he yelled out. "Retreat!"

The Shadow Warriors formed a circle around the Seventh Council convoy, immediately casting a shield to protect them.

"We have come to beat the beasts back," Düsternis shouted, fixing Winter with a lethal glare. "Perhaps our personal differences can wait."

"In that case, welcome to hell," Winter shouted back.

The warriors split and rejoined the fight. More monsters poured into the forest, enclosing us in a ring of beaks, fangs, talons and claws. I held the shield steady to protect the Valkyries from the scent phantoms as they worked like a well-tuned machine, using blade and bow to dispatch monster after monster to the afterlife.

The white snow on the ground turned dark with beast blood as the Immortal blades mowed them down. There was no hesitation in the eyes of the creatures as they fell onto the swords, unconcerned with certain death.

I freed my sword from its sheath. Rage rose inside my etheric core as I crashed into the fray. It took a lot of energy to keep the shield going while I fought, but the enchanted forest offered unlimited supplies. My sword swung down hard, thirsty for blood. The monsters must have sensed the eternal blood in my veins because they were unwilling to engage me.

You bastards, was it Horror who instructed you not to touch me?

I gave chase to the beasts, my sword slicing through hides, surging on anger and adrenaline.

Suddenly, more beasts pulled back, fleeing the blood-stained battlefield. The scent phantoms vanished. The ground quaked. Huge branches bent down like wooden arms with a hundred jagged edges to sweep the forest clean with incredible speed. Any still standing on the ground would be harpooned with naked branches and quickly disemboweled.

We ducked and ran, breaking formation. The beasts crashed into each other, the morphs ripping through the other monsters frantically to get away from the bloody sweep of the deadly branches.

The humongous bat creatures plunged down at us in a demonic frenzy. Blades whizzed and hummed through the air, followed by painful wails as they carved through the creatures.

A wave of magic rolled across the battlefield, silencing the fighters. A portal opened with a pop and started to spew out an endless number of new demons. The trees settled and the scent phantoms returned.

I wiped sweat from my brow. This wasn't going to work. There was no end to the beasts who kept joining the battle. No matter how many we slaughtered, there'd be more coming, then still more and more. To leave now would be granting them access to Muir Woods and the basic world. To keep fighting, would mean we'd stay trapped in here with them forever, our numbers slowly dwindling.

I took a deep breath. When the time portal had opened, I'd managed to anchor some ley line energy inside it.

It was a huge risk, but a necessary one. I scanned the forest for Winter. He was fighting a huge, scaled buffalo from hell with his bare hands. That thing looked like a work in progress as it kept mutating into possibly a triceratops or ankylosaurus or some other form of dinosaur.

Winter punched the beast again and again with one hand, the other hand locked on one of its horns. The buffalo breathed fire out of its nostrils. It pressed forward, trying to ram Winter. Winter's muscles bulged, but he kept the beast immobile.

Alright, he's got this.

The stream of monsters kept flowing. Our fighters gave it everything they had, but their stamina and strength were not limitless. They could not hold.

The enchanted forest swelled with magic. I inhaled it all, letting it fill my lungs and my core to full capacity. I dropped the force field and with it the cloaking of my etheric essence. To perform the colossal task ahead, I needed my magic out in the open, freed of all shackles and all protections.

I pulled more magic to me. I pulled it from the frozen trees, the pale slice of moonlight penetrating the foliage, the ley line intersection, the snowflakes, the lingering hedge witchcraft, and even the beasts themselves. My energy core had become a sponge, absorbing everything it came in contact with, stretching to maximum capacity.

My magic boomed in my ears, melding with the eternal fire that now flowed through me. I wondered if that was how Horror felt every day of his life: intoxicated by his own power.

Magic shot out of me like a roaring waterfall. The colossal trees shuddered. The ground rumbled with seismic violence. The hordes of beasts shivered, caught in the whirlpool of my magic.

Rings of golden energy raced upwards to hook onto the ley line energy I'd placed inside the portal, shattering its cloaking. The time portal materialized above me. I poured oodles of magic inside it, opening it wide.

My teeth chattered with the effort. I realized that every being was staring at me. The ranks of morphs and creatures and phantoms were swept off their feet, collapsing into the hissing time portal in a mass of bent limbs and twisted necks.

The pain kicked in, hot and agonizing. It was as if someone was shoving thick needles in my temples, my stomach and my chest. Too much magic too quickly. The pressure shredded my core. My breathing turned shallow.

I saw Winter's face, distorted with concern. He yelled something, but all I could hear was the buzz in my ears. An opposing force was pushing back with incredible intensity, blocking my energy.

I just have to hold on a little longer.

The time portal spun away from my control. When it opened again, it was to unleash the newest horde of monstrosities.

A hand landed on my shoulder. I turned. "Are you okay?" Kirsi asked. The Valkyrie was bathed in blood. "Luna? Answer me!"

An eerie howl rang through the forest. Something else fell from the sky. It wasn't a monster, or maybe it was the biggest monster of them all.

Horror.

Tall, clad in shiny armor, with red hair glowing like fire, he stomped onto the battlefield like he owned it. A silver axe flashed in his hand. A slight grin curled his lips. His aura was golden. Horror looked like a mythical god.

He screamed like a madman at the beasts.

Blades clanked and whistled, pointing at my father. Shadow Warriors, Valkyries and Magistrates, all knew who he was, and they wanted to capture him.

Horror thrust the axe above his head. "Daddy's here," he said.

His axe swung above his head in circles. The time portal stilled. The beasts got caught in a forceful vortex spiraling upwards. We watched as the time portal absorbed them at a dizzying speed. My father's magic whipped around me, entering my bloodstream, feeding me with new energy. The sky turned a bright red like it was bleeding. The time portal vanished and with it all our opponents.

The cold intensified. Frost licked at the skin on my face. In my mind, there was relief but also wariness. Somehow, in some place deep within, part of me hoped Horror wasn't the puppeteer who pulled the monsters' strings. Part of me hoped he wasn't all horrible and I wouldn't have to fight him.

Horror's energy shield became visible, a solid wall of magnetic forces fortified with wards forged with his own blood. I knew there was no force in the universe that could break or penetrate that shield.

Winter closed the distance between us with long strides, plodding through the carnage on the forest floor. His face was a mask of menace, his eyes fixated on Horror.

My father dropped his shield. His gaze landed on Winter. "Chief Magistrate, we've met once before, have we not? In the Eternal Halls if I recall? I find it curious, and forgive me if I'm overstepping, that you would fight side by side with the woman who killed your infant son. I know I could not allow that."

And there it was. The reason why we had all bled in this enchanted forest, the reason why so many banished creatures had to die cruel deaths. So that Horror could have his grand theatrical moment at Winter's expense.

Winter stared at Horror, uncomprehending. Chazona backed away, her face paler than the frost.

"Don't," I told Horror. "Stop your games."

"You don't know?" Horror went on, feigning surprise. "That woman over there, Magistrate Chazona, she orchestrated the accident that cost your little boy and his mother their lives. Now if it were me, I would not want her anywhere near my lovely new woman."

I took Winter's hand and squeezed. He yanked his hand away. His face had the resigned determination of a man who had lost everything. In my heart, I knew this was a moment that would haunt us forever. I would never forget it, because I had to remember that no matter what my father said, he was the biggest asshole in all the realms.

Winter's pain pulsed through my veins. My body ached for him.

He pushed me aside and pounced on Horror. It happened so fast I felt frozen in place. Winter howled like a wounded predator and rammed Horror, flinging him against a tree trunk.

My worst fears realized.

Horror bounced back onto his feet. A satisfied smirk curled his lips for a split second before Winter charged him again, his big fist slamming into Horror's throat, shattering his windpipe.

A ghastly holler gushed out of Horror's throat. His face twisted into pure rage. He charged Winter, smashing into him and knocking him off his feet.

I realized both their shields were down. They wanted this fight gory and brutal.

The idiots!

Winter twisted out of Horror's clutch and leaped away. Horror lunged after him. Winter got out of the way just in time, so Horror's fist pommeled an enchanted redwood, bashing an arm-sized hole into the trunk.

The warriors watched the battle of titans enthralled. I noticed someone was missing. Düsternis. For some reason, Chazona was still here. The ice queen had zero sense in her evil little head.

Winter's eyes glowed with a murderous zeal. Eventually Horror would tire of this game and then the man I loved would be in lethal danger.

I jumped smack dab in the middle of the fight, just as Winter ripped a huge branch off a redwood and readied to crush Horror's skull. He swung the branch just as I landed in front of him. He reversed course instantly, but the edge of the branch gashed into my left arm.

Fucking ow!

Horror landed a kick that sent Winter flying.

"Stop, just stop," I yelled. "You utter morons, stop it already!"

Horror shook his head trying to shake the cobwebs out. Winter punched a tree causing his knuckles to bleed. He roared so loud snow fell from the branches above. He ran off into the darkness of the forest.

Horror tried to follow after him. I blocked his way. "Don't you even dare. Not now, not ever."

All eyes fell on me once again. Eyebrows crept up inquisitively.

Yeah, I just commanded Horror. Get over it.

All that anger in me, I had to put it somewhere.

"Why?" I asked Chazona. "You could have any man you want. Why did you have to break his soul for eternity?"

Chazona's mask slipped off her face. Her expression turned sour. "You think I did it for love, you silly twat?" She laughed. "The Grand Magistrate could feel Winter giving way to sickly human emotions. Our Chief Magistrate had decided to play house with an insignificant mortal. His break from reality would put us all at risk. A correction needed to be made."

I couldn't hear that bitch anymore. It sounded like a slew of Magistrates had been behind the murders. I looked to Kirsi. "Make sure they all pay."

"I'm handling her," Horror said. "Already chained her core to me."

Ah, that's why she hasn't fled.

I turned and ran into the winter woods chasing after Winter.

Chapter 22

The wintry night in the enchanted forest was full of terrors. Hundreds of morphs were dead, and maybe thousands of supernatural creatures once banished. Mangled corpses had found their way among the frozen trees hundreds of yards away from the battleground. They lay on trampled earth atop each other, against rocks, over fallen trunks, snow already falling on them, freezing instantly as it mixed with the darkening blood of death.

Exhaustion was starting to sink into my body. My legs felt heavy like I'd just finished a marathon. Every muscle and bone hurt in many new and excruciating ways.

The haze of a bonfire rose to my left, rising all the way to the treetops. Its warmth soothed me, coating my iced face like hot chocolate. Someone or something howled—a wolf maybe or a man in pain. My skin prickled.

I remembered Winter's words. The forest magic was

illusive and evocative and fed on memories and fears. My head spun with both—memories of a brutal battle that had drained my core and fear of losing Winter to his renewed grief.

Why did Horror desire to torture me with elaborate schemes? Couldn't he just challenge me to a battle to death? Did he really have to destroy everyone around me because I cherished them more than I did him?

"Winter," I whispered. "Where are you?"

A distant, eerie voice whispered back. *Winter lives in the woods.*

The dark hissed and sizzled. My words must have summoned a vision. A dark wooden door appeared in front of me; ice shards crackled as the door slowly opened. Flames fizzed and spat in the fireplace inside a cabin. A string of lights flickered on a glossy-green Christmas tree, coloring the silver tinsel with blues and reds and yellows. A holiday tune rang out from the back of the house. *Jingle bells, jingle bells, jingle all the way.*

A heap of snow slid off the top of a tree and landed at my feet. The vision vanished. The frost surrounded me, more vicious than before.

My heart sank. Winter's tracks stretched far into the icy forest path, half covered by the falling snow. If I didn't hurry up, I might lose him forever.

I rubbed my arms together for warmth. My breath froze upon touching the air. A tall figure appeared in a gap between two redwoods. He was half-naked, unbothered by the cold, bits of frost gleaming on his chest. Smears of blood were visible on his face and arms, his frozen hair caked with gore. The wounds from his removed tattoos were now gone. A golden glow pulsed inside his glacial, cruel eyes.

Winter had gone completely feral, his humanity vanished.

"It's me," I whispered, stupidly. "I'm Luna."

"I know who you are," he said and walked right past me.

I followed behind. "You said you are not afraid of pain. You said you're not driven by emotion," I reminded him. "So, what the hell? Did you want Horror to kill you? Would you give him that satisfaction?"

Sparks surged in his fingertips. "Not all things answer to reason."

"It's over, now let's go home."

My plea fell on deaf ears. He looked past me. "Some things are never over, Luna Mae. Some things linger forevermore."

I reached out to take his arm. "Come with me, Winter."

He stopped and looked at me. "I can't."

With every beat of my heart, I felt his pain ticking like a bomb. I didn't know how to take that pain away. I did not have that power.

"Please," I said. "We can talk it out, talk about everything. We can talk and talk, Winter. We can talk forever. I should have told you everything, but I was never sure, not really, and I didn't want to hurt you. I didn't want you to live through it all over again."

Winter narrowed his eyes as he considered my words. I expected to find anger in those eyes, but what I found resembled sadness and resignation.

"You knew," he said. "All this time you knew, and you said nothing. Which means, it is all true. My boy and Helen died at Chazona's hands."

"It's more complicated than one person, but yes, Horror left clues for me and Kirsi. We couldn't know for sure. It's not something to get wrong."

He laughed now, his shoulders shaking. I feared he had gone mad. "My faithful Valkyrie and my loving mist rider," he said. "My two most trusted allies and dearest friends, conspiring to keep me in the dark."

"It's not like that and you know it. I had every intention of telling you what we knew so far, but then I saw you with Chazona, how you trusted her and considered her a friend, and I knew the truth would break you."

"Stupid little fools," he said, failing to contain his contempt. "You thought you could hide a secret that Horror knew? And what, you would let me continue to confide in Chazona, exposing my weaknesses, giving her insight into your whereabouts so she could strike again?"

"When you say it like that, it sounds dumb, but when Kirsi and I started investigating the possibility, you were still at Darius's camp, in recovery mode. We hadn't planned on you getting home so quickly, this was a project to be worked on for years while you were sleeping. We didn't know what to do. Horror could have manipulated us and Chazona could have been innocent."

"The minute I woke, these were not your decisions to make."

"I realize that. I'm sorry. I overstepped."

"Luna Mae overstepping..." he said, shrugging. "It's what you do."

Sure, but...

He walked off. I ran past him to grab his chin and turn his face to me. "Jonas, I'm sorry, okay, I messed up. I'm not perfect, I know, big revelation. Why don't you realize I'm a work in progress? My heart was in the right place. I wanted to protect you. I tried to be like you, carry the burden of uncertain truths, protect you from the weight of it until the time was right. I'm just beginning in this world. I'm trying to love you."

He struggled with that for a moment. "Don't try to be me," he said. "That doesn't even work for me. I know you tried to do right, and I know you're a neophyte in this world. But now this is mine to deal with in my way."

"And your way involves staying away from me?" My voice came out more bitter than I intended. I wrapped my arms around his naked torso, pulling him to me. "Let me love you, Jonas. We can figure things out together."

He cupped my hands with his, unfastening my grip. "I have felt those things for you, but right now I am nothing and have nothing to give."

Winter stepped over the corpse of a bat-bear and trotted ahead, leaving me behind. We had come full circle. I had walked away from him so many times unable to forgive, and now, it seemed, he was doing the same.

I sucked in a sob. "Be safe! Don't forget who your friends are. Kirsi loves you. Let her help you at least. I made her do everything! Jonas, don't forget where you belong!"

He turned back. "I don't forget. I remember everything. Kirsi is forgiven. Now you go home, go to where you belong, Sophie. Don't follow."

Winter disappeared as if never there. I stood alone in the enchanted forest, surrounded by a moonlight mist, wondering if it had all been a vision, that maybe all of life is a vision, maybe we are all madmen stuck in the woods on a winter's night.

My hands were numb from the cold, my nose raw from frostbite. Around me, snowflakes swirled about in a dance of loneliness.

I wanted to scream. I wanted to tear my skin away and be as naked as he was in this cold, never-ending world.

My eyes closed in the frozen dark. I saw Winter clearly for the first time. A child born in a faraway fjord of ice, a man who walked alone through the world cloaked in dark secrets and timeless heartaches, a warrior who fought gods and demons alike. For the first time, I felt him.

A broken man defending a broken world.

Chapter 23

A WEEK LATER

I knocked on Emmet's door, my heart accelerating as I squeezed the white wine bottle in my hands.

Emmet pulled the door open dressed in jeans, t-shirt and an apron. The gravelly voice of Tom Waits sang in the background.

"A doctor who can cook," I said, arching an eyebrow. "Is there anything you don't do, Dr. Groshek?"

Emmet set my bottle on the counter. "No, I do it all. All thanks to my inferiority complex."

"I assumed you'd order from some place."

"Tsk, tsk," he said as he folded his apron. "Haven't you heard?" He leaned in and whispered, "Shifters are excellent cooks."

I panicked. "Dude, be quiet... is she here yet?"

Emmet nodded. "In the bathroom and you need to chill."

"Did you have a chance to talk to her?"

"Of course, but she really wants to hear your side of the story."

I sighed. This night was surreal. Meeting with Lily again after the Savroid incident felt like a first date with a guy way out of my league. No matter what I did, I was going to blow it.

I'm the worst blind date ever.

Lily walked into the room. I gulped; my hands felt clammy. Normally, she would light up with a mischievous flare in her eyes when she saw me. Not today. Today she looked pale and fatigued, her eyes haunted. I could tell that she had lost a few pounds. Her face brightened for a breath when she saw me and then deflated.

I smiled, sheepishly. We both had had better weeks, but we managed to look at each other at least, trying to be pleasant.

Yuck, that's not us.

"You look like crap," Lily said, not without some effort.

"You look worse," I said.

"I have to warn you," she said, pointing at Emmet. "All his towels and linen are white. He's Hannibal Lector neat."

"And he likes to cook," I said. "This is bad."

Emmet's face went red before shaking his head. "That didn't take long," he said. "And, I promise, no humans were hurt in the making of this meal."

Emmet sat opposite me, with Lily next to him. His gentle, confident manner always put my mind at ease. Little by little,

I found myself relaxing. I searched his eyes for reassurance that Lily would be okay—that we all would.

Emmet had prepared pork chops with a mushroom sauce, risotto and a tomato cucumber salad. Everything tasted delicious. He poured the wine in tall glasses as we ate mostly in silence.

I fixed my eyes on Lily. "Emmet told you a tall tale?"

Lily put her fork down. "I think he has a drinking problem. He told me incredible, ridiculous stories of a supernatural world, witches, fae and demons. I think he's a Comic Con nerd. I chose to believe him because he's kind of yum and annoyingly nice."

"His sincerity wears you down," I agreed.

Lily looked down at her hands. "Any other of my homies turn into ponies or Cinderella or anything?"

"Faion," I said. "Also, my gram. It's usually a peaceful, quiet world, Lily. We're not monsters. I'm still Sophie Collinsworth, the dork you met freshman year who always tried for extra credit. I grew up just like you, only recently have things gone a little sideways and I chip in with a zap or two."

Her eyes teared up. "These aren't tears," she said. "My eyes are just sweating. You could have told me, Sophie. I can keep a secret. Did I ever tell anyone about that guy in the bathroom at the Ed Sheeran concert?"

Emmet's eyes opened wide.

"She made that up, Emmet," I said. "It was two guys."

"I get it though," Lily said.

"Oh, honey, I wanted to tell you, but we take an oath. The two worlds are never supposed to mingle, Lil."

She gave me a labored smile. "You saved my life, I know that. I saw it in your face, Sophie. You would have died to protect me."

I leaned over and kissed Lily on the forehead. "Of course, I would. And you would do the same."

She grabbed my hand and stared deep into my eyes. "That was a close call," she said, letting out emotions she may have saved for me and hid from her mother and Emmet.

Emmet stood up. "Something in the kitchen." He left.

"I know, baby girl, but it's over now," I said, going around the table to hug her beautiful head. "If we can take anything from this mess, it's that we truly love each other."

"And we're ride-or-die bitches?" she said, lightly sobbing.

"Yes, we are most def ride-or-die bitches," I agreed, brushing her hair back away from her tears.

"I knew it," she said, quietly. She lowered her eyes. "Every sound startles me."

My tears streamed down now. "I know, it gets better. You have some badass friends that can really watch out for you."

"My friends are so badass," she said, then sat up, recomposing herself.

Emmet returned with a tissue box each.

"Damn it, Emmet," Lily said, "why'd you use all those onions?"

He reached over and took Lily's hand. *What now?* Those hands looked familiar with each other. They had grown close. Maybe it was a good thing. Maybe Emmet was the perfect man for her, for any woman. It was a selfish thought. After all, if Lily had his wolf babies, she'd have no room to judge.

Lily stared at the fork in her hand for a while. "I've been thinking," she said. "Everything seems clear now. I needed something big to happen, something to get me out of my funk, you know, before I let life pass me by."

"I'll start you on a monster a day diet," Emmet said.

"Emmet," I said, training my fork on him.

Lily laughed. I knew exactly how she felt. There was no looking back.

"We can't keep living in the past," she said. "We have to move on. I have to find out who I really am and make sure I live a life that matters."

So proud of her. Am I sure I'm not a lesbian?

"You were always going to do that, Silly Lily," I said. "But you are being so fierce right now that you're giving me young Oprah vibes."

"Uh-uh," she said. "You're fiercer than anyone. You're the *fiercest* of the fiercest. You got that Captain-Mar-vel-Brie-Larsson vibe. It's so hot. You're a goddamned su-perhero, sis. What else can you do?"

"It looks colorful," I said, shaking my head, "but it's all just security guard type shit to keep everything smooth. It's a real bummer for makeup and I never get to wear any clothes I care about. A lot of gross and messy work. And did I say, zero pay, zip, nothing, no union, not even a bathroom break. It's a whole drama and it's boring to be honest."

"Nice try," she said. "I'm going to need actual gossip eventually. None of that humble brag business you just tried to pull."

"Fine, but you're really okay, Lil?"

"I wasn't injured, thanks to you. And I wasn't fine before, so I'm good. Real terror was definitely a whole new mood though. I'll work through all that, it's part of my exciting new world."

"We'll work through this, and through men and every other vile thing life throws at us," I said. "Our pity parties have the best snacks."

Lily's face took on a guilty quality. "I told Emmet I'll need to get the international call plan for just this reason. I want to hear your voice."

"What do you mean international call plan?"

Lily beamed. "Emmet finally gave in. He's totally taking me on his long Greek adventure."

My heart sank. *I'm the worst friend.*

"Seriously?" I said, surprised that Emmet had not only decided to take that fake trip after all but also agreed to take Lily along. I could guess how she persuaded him.

That total sl-- Nope, rise above, Sophie.

"Yes, quite serious," Lily said, imitating Emmet (*I think*).

Beyond the selfish need to have my best friend close, I also had a lot of questions for them both, but I guess their happiness trumped my needs.

"Now you have to get me drunk," I said with a deep sigh. "So, I don't get super selfish about everyone leaving me at once."

MY BODY FELT NUMB from head to toe, my soul lagging. The sudden absence of all purpose and direction hit me hard. After a year of manic action, I now had nothing to do. I lingered outside my door, key in hand. I had a nice time with Lily and Emmet, but now I was drunk and had to face an empty apartment.

I had decided to let Winter go, to set him free for as long as he needed. The best thing I could do for him was back off, but it stung.

Ugh, I shouldn't have slowed down my metabolism to get drunk.

With a sigh, I unlocked my door. Stepping inside I was immediately hit by pungent magic like a punch in the face.

Horror sat on my couch, wrapped up in one of my blankets.

I turned off the cheerful cooking show on my television.

He woke up, stretching his arms above his head. "I must have dozed off."

This can't be happening.

"What do you want, dad I never asked for?"

He frowned. "I want you to get a full-length couch. These half-sized ones seem like a cruel tease if I'm being honest."

"You are known for your honesty," I said, rolling my eyes. "And so why have you darkened my doorstep? As you can see, I don't have any Immortal buddies here for you to psychologically destroy."

"I missed my daughter," he said. "A father can't stay away for long."

Exactly what's worrying me.

"Alright," I said. "Since you're here, can you explain what motive you had to tell Winter about Chazona in that cruel, selfish way? You knew he was high on adrenaline and basically drunk on magic. We were all kind of busy."

His face turned expressionless, but he couldn't fool me. He was pissed. "That woman disrespected you again and again with no respect for your bloodline," he said. "She had to face consequences."

So, there it was. It was all about him, his fucking bloodline.

"And you orchestrated the whole slaughter fest as a backdrop?"

Horror stood. "Daughter," he said, his voice booming. "I have told you before, but this time you are going to believe me. I had nothing to do with the beasts or the time portals. I came to your aid because I know when you're in the thick of it. That's the whole story. So let go of the nonsense."

He opened his hand. I placed my hand in Horror's palm. A connective path linked us like a shooting arrow, opening a searing stream of energy between us. His magic collided with mine, drilling down into my etheric essence. Wild vibrations pooled in my blood. Horror squeezed my hand. I peeked inside his beating heart. I saw truth there.

Horror removed his hand. The connection extinguished and I gasped.

"See, my bloom, your father does not lie."

Okay, he hadn't lied in the strictest sense of the word, but he had advanced ways to manipulate. He had easily slithered his way into my life and had planted doubt in my mind. Not only that, by defeating Darius, I had effectively won Horror's war for him.

"If not you, who then?" I said. "Was it all Darius?"

"Perhaps, but he has a sub lieutenant, that much is plain."

"Who?"

"Some fool who will soon regret it. I'll crack the riddle soon enough."

"Here's a plan," I said. "Leave and come back when you have something."

"Fair enough, I have read, in this world, it's best not to cramp your child's style by hanging around too much. I'll step back, give you your time but, Luna, there is much to do, and time's always wasting."

Horror walked to the door. He turned back. "Interesting tidbit," he said. "The performance issue you're having with your male friend, the deafening reverberations of your union..."

Ew. "Please, father, stop. So gross."

He got serious. "I was just saying, that's all on him."

I opened the door. He mercifully left.

Now I was dizzy, nauseous and confused. No, forget that. I refused to be confused about Winter. Whatever he was... I was down with it. All the haters had to stop talking shit about my man.

I needed to lie down. It had been a day.

Chapter 24

A MONTH LATER

A COOL EVENING BREEZE hit my skin from the open window. I walked around my small apartment with a strained smile, picking up dirty dishes.

"Don't mind me," I whispered to a spider hanging from the ceiling in my kitchen as I grabbed a water bottle from the fridge.

I made my way to the couch. I undressed quickly and slipped into some lounge pants and an oversized t-shirt. The night called for some chocolate cake in front of the TV.

Pro level spinster moves.

I needed to find something not real, something in another time and century, another world, some place dark and mysterious, but where I'm not the one getting smacked and covered in gunk. I wanted to feel safe and snug on my couch.

I settled down deciding to binge watch the first season of

Vikings when the doorbell rang.

My heart fluttered like a hummingbird. I knew that it was Winter.

He was undone when I opened the door. Sweat soaked through his workout shirt and his hair was moist and disheveled. He had a hungry, lost look on his perspiring face.

"I was in the neighborhood," he said.

I just stared at him. *What is happening right now?*

"Will you let me in?"

"Have you been running?"

You can't be serious, Luna. That's your great comeback?

"I was at the gym," he said. "We have to talk."

He let himself in and walked straight to the kitchen. I watched him gulp down my last bottle of water. He wiped his mouth with the back of his hand.

Maybe I fell asleep on the couch and I'm dreaming.

"I'm sorry," I said. "Can you pinch me?"

He pinched my arm without a second thought. Hard. *Ouch.*

"So, which is it? Were you in the neighborhood or were you at the gym? I don't think there's a gym in the neighborhood," I said, because I'm the Queen of saying stupid things.

Winter studied my face. His eyes were void of emotion. Instead, he looked at me like I was in his way somehow. He stepped to me suddenly. My heart thumped so fast as I sensed something dangerous inside him.

His next step brought his powerful body against mine. My

skin began to panic and tingle. My hands shook a little as they landed on his chest. I felt physically overwhelmed.

"What are you doing here?" I said, struggling to keep my head straight.

"I bathed inside the cathartic eternal springs of my homeland," he said.

"That sounds very cool, but…"

"The eternal springs cleansed my etheric essence," he said. "They cleared my vision and my spirit, Luna Mae. Kirsi joined me. I wasn't sure it was going to work, but I needed to move away from the darkness."

"Um, you should do that more often," I said. "Can I do it?"

He smiled. "It involves a great deal of pain." He leaned closer. "You smell like chocolate." He licked the corner of my lips. "You taste like chocolate, too."

"If you hadn't told me a hundred times sex is out of the question, I'd say you dropped by for a booty call."

Yes, please.

His eyes grew wild underneath the fluorescent light—his pupils widened as he stared down at me like a voracious predator. I felt naked. He saw right through me. He sensed my fears. He felt my desires.

A sigh escaped my lips and then my mouth found his in an urgent, possessive, delicious tangle of tongues.

"I never expected this," he said. "Your light guided me back to your door, Luna Mae. Your light saved me."

"Women fall for these lines?" I said, trying to lighten the mood.

"I don't know," he said, softly nibbling on my earlobe, sending tremors down my spine. "I've never talked like that."

"Okay, I choose to fall for that line."

A smile curled his lips. "Just be quiet," he said as he took both my wrists in one hand, raising them above my head to pin me against my kitchen wall.

I stared up into his eyes. "I thought we couldn't get physical. Like ever."

He arched an eyebrow. "Oh, no. That was bullshit."

What? "Remember, when we were trapped in the inverse energy reactor? We blew the whole damn thing to smithereens."

"The cleansing process," he said. "For a few days, while my etheric essence and my energy core restore, my cells will be mortal."

His mouth got busy with my lips, ears and neck. He let go of my wrists to free both hands so they could roam my body.

The world began to spin. His fevered affection moved everywhere at once, exploring. His touch warmed me like a velvety fire racing over my skin.

I pulled his mouth down to mine, needing to taste him, wanting to savor every moment. Everything inside of me turned to hot jelly.

"Take me to bed," I commanded.

He carried me with one arm around my back and the other

under my knees.

This was happening. Finally. I wrapped my arms around his neck as he hurried to the bed. He laid me down slowly, his eyes never leaving mine. He was as needy now as I was which was a scandalous amount.

He smiled, tracing the contours of my face with a gentle knuckle. He placed kisses on my eyelids and my nose and my lips. I purred. For real.

Now his finger followed the path of my collarbone as his lips sucked on my earlobe. Too much. I was drowning in pleasurable impulses. Too many to separate or describe. If I were a chameleon, I'd be a hundred shades of sparkling glitter. My frantic heartbeat felt as combustible and infinite as a million dying stars.

Winter lifted the hem of my shirt above my belly, planting a kiss on my ribs. I arched my back and moaned, helpless.

My brain turned to mush, my very core about to ignite. His legs straddled my legs as he hovered above me. He lowered himself, pressing his body against mine. My heart frenzied with anticipation.

"I want to own your senses," he said as he kissed me. "Unlock every pleasurable treasure."

I smiled. "Knock yourself out," I said breathlessly.

So, that happened. I slept with Winter last night. Multiple times. Not only that, but he also now slept in my bed with no intention of leaving. I still felt dizzy from the whiplash of his sudden magnificence.

I stepped out of the shower, patting the towel all over my naked body to dry my skin. I took one last look in the mirror. I had just had the best sex of my life and the world was left standing. My pale skin glowed brighter and my eyes had a new determination in them as I could feel my own life force burgeoning positively within.

A quick knock sounded through the apartment. I quickly wrapped my robe around me and stepped out of the bathroom. Chaos stood at the doorstep. He held out his hand to poke at my wards. He was in a sour mood, more so than usual.

"We need to talk," he said.

"Meet me in ten minutes at the Starbucks down the street."

"How about a nice mountaintop?"

I didn't get a chance to respond. Chaos crushed my wards and hugged me tight. A flash of blue smoke spun around us and the next thing I knew, I was on a fucking mountaintop. Barefoot and wrapped in a bathrobe.

"I'm sorry," Chaos said. "I couldn't risk Horror listening in through your pretty little head."

"Chaos, what's this all about?"

"You're not going to like it."

"Just spit it out."

A shadow passed from his face. "Your mother, they call her Time. She is the ultimate chronomaster. She can alter the course of time without creating looping paradoxes. She can lock and unlock time at will, like placing it in a box and keeping it outside the flow of history. I'm not even sure how it works, but there you have it. She's a lot."

"Why are you telling me this? Why now?" I said, the darkest premonitions flooding my mind.

"Because she is the one opening the time portals and releasing unspeakable beasts onto us. Your mother has been working with Darius."

"No," I said. "You are wrong. I must have at least one parent who's not a complete lunatic and a scourge on humanity."

"That's not Time," he said. "She's powerful and ambitious, yes, but she is not one ounce evil. There is more to this story than what we can see, I'm certain of that."

"You always do that, don't you? Defend her, do her bidding. Has it crossed your mind she has been using you?"

He pondered that for a moment. "Listen closely. Horror cannot know any of this. He is unpredictable when it comes to her."

"Time?"

"Yes, Time. It'd be best never to poke that hornet's nest. Not now."

Or ever.

"So, what do we do?" I said.

"I will take you to her," Chaos said. "Let me arrange it."

Suddenly my entire body went cold. An overwhelming physical dread ached in my every joint and nerve.

"Why do I feel so overwhelmed?"

"To say her name out loud in your presence," he said, hesitantly, "it triggers timeless pathways coded into your cells."

"Brother," I said, "you seem so unsure of yourself. I have never seen you like this. What does it all mean?"

He pushed back my hair and smiled to me like a young boy.

"It means, dear sister, that the real war, the only war and the final war for the realms is about to begin."

About the Author

Stella Fitzsimons was born in Athens, Greece, and lives in Southern California with her husband and two sons. After studying economics and language arts she went on to teach both Mathematics and English before launching *Stella's Literary Bistro*, a bilingual literary journal. Her works include: *The Vanishing Tome, Luna, Winter, Silver Dust, Shadow Fall, Moonlight Mist* and *The Last Rider.*